# "PERFECT. YOU HAD TO MAKE THIS HARDER, DIDN'T YOU?"

Cordy sounded annoyed, of all things.

"Okay," Xander said slowly. "Clearly the fact that I please you visually has got us off on the wrong foot here."

"Xander—" she started.

He handed her the gift box.

Cordelia took the box and opened it. "Xander, thank you." She took out the necklace. "It's beautiful." Then she lowered the chain into the box and said, "I want to break up."

Xander somehow managed not to scream. "Okay, not quite the reaction I was looking for."

"I know. I'm sorry," Cordy said, and for once in her life, she sounded sincere. "It's just—who are we kidding? We don't fit."

A small part of Xander saw this coming. A lifetime of rejection had prepared him for this moment.

*But not tonight. Of all nights, not tonight.*

"Yeah, okay," he said, trying and failing to keep his temper. "You know what's a good day to break up with somebody? Any day besides Valentine's Day! I mean, what, were you just running low on dramatic irony?"

**Buffy the Vampire Slayer™**

Buffy the Vampire Slayer (movie tie-in)
The Harvest
Halloween Rain
Coyote Moon
Night of the Living Rerun
The Angel Chronicles, Vol. 1
Blooded
The Angel Chronicles, Vol. 2
The Xander Years, Vol. 1

Available from ARCHWAY Paperbacks

**Buffy the Vampire Slayer adult books**

Child of the Hunt
Return to Chaos
The Gatekeeper Trilogy
  Book 1: Out of the Madhouse

The Watcher's Guide: The Official Companion to the Hit Show

Available from POCKET BOOKS

# BUFFY
## THE VAMPIRE
# SLAYER™

## THE XANDER YEARS

### Vol. 1

A novelization by Keith R.A. DeCandido
Based on the hit TV series created by Joss Whedon
Based on the teleplays "Teacher's Pet" by David Greenwalt,
"Inca Mummy Girl" by Matt Kiene & Joe Reinkemeyer,
and "Bewitched, Bothered & Bewildered" by Marti Noxon

POCKET BOOKS
New York   London   Toronto   Sydney   Tokyo   Singapore

This book is a work of fiction. Names, characters, places and incidents are products of the author's imagination or are used fictitiously. Any resemblance to actual events or locales or persons, living or dead, is entirely coincidental.

AN ARCHWAY PAPERBACK *Original*

An Archway Paperback published by
POCKET BOOKS, a division of Simon & Schuster Inc.
1230 Avenue of the Americas, New York, NY 10020

™ and copyright © 1999 by Twentieth Century Fox Film Corporation. All rights reserved.

All rights reserved, including the right to reproduce this book or portions thereof in any form whatsoever. For information address Pocket Books, 1230 Avenue of the Americas, New York, NY 10020

ISBN: 0-671-02629-1

First Archway Paperback printing February 1999

10  9  8  7  6  5  4  3  2  1

AN ARCHWAY PAPERBACK and colophon are registered trademarks of Simon & Schuster Inc.

Printed in the U.S.A.

IL: 9+

This book is dedicated to Alexander LaVelle Harris, a hero to all us high-school geeks, and also to Joss Whedon, who gave him life, and to Nicholas Brendon, who gave him form and substance.

# ACKNOWLEDGMENTS

Primary thanks have to go to *Buffy* creator/executive producer Joss Whedon, whose fault this all is, as well as David Greenwalt and Bruce Seth Green (who wrote and directed "Teacher's Pet"), Matt Kiene and Joe Reinkemeyer and Ellen S. Pressman ("Inca Mummy Girl"), and Marti Noxon and James A. Contner ("Bewitched, Bothered, and Bewildered"; my one regret in this book is that I could not do justice in prose to the magnificent "Got the Love" scene in this episode, for which I most heartily commend Ms. Noxon and Mr. Conter).

Huge thanks of course go to my editor, the magnificent Lisa Clancy, and her assistant, the equally magnificent Elizabeth Shiflett, for the opportunity to work on the book and for answering all my stupid and annoying questions. Huge thanks also to Christopher Golden and Nancy Holder, for opening several doors, and to Laura Anne Gilman, for being both best editor and best friend.

Not-so-huge (but still pretty big) thanks go to the following: John C. Bunnell, Livia DeCandido, John S. Drew, Brandy Hauman, Orenthal V. Hawkins, Alexandra Elizabeth Honigsberg, David M. Honigsberg,

# ACKNOWLEDGMENTS

Dori Koogler, Julianne Lee, Andrea K. Lipinski, Peter Liverakos, Dave Logsdon, James Macdonald, Ashley McConnell, Sue Phillips, Kimberley Rector, the gang on Buffy-L@planetx.com, and the entire Malibu Lunch Crowd.

And finally the biggest thanks of them all go to my lovely and much more talented wife, Marina Frants, and to the Forebearance: the Mom (who also provided mucho editorial input), the Dad, John, and Helga.

# TONIGHT, PART 1

The argument started when Cordelia saw what Xander was wearing.

He had only just walked into the Bronze when Cordy started in on him. "My *God*, what is that outfit?"

"It's called 'clothes.'"

"No, *I'm* wearing clothes. *You* are wearing rags. Xander, do you even know what it means to accessorize?"

Shaking his head and rolling his eyes at the same time, Xander replied, "Yeah. *To accessorize.* A verb deriving from the noun *accessory.* Loosely defined as, 'Caring way more about what you're wearing than is necessary for simple human interpersonal contact.'"

Gesturing as if she were pleading with Xander to

not jump off a high ledge, Cordelia said, "Xander, clothes are what define who you are to the world. They put out a message that says, 'I'm cool' or 'I'm a jock' or 'I'm a computer geek' or, in your case, 'I'm a loser with no redeeming social value.'"

It went downhill from there, at least up to the part where they made up by necking near the restrooms.

Xander returned home and fell more than sat on his bed, not even bothering to clear a space for himself—he just collapsed onto the dirty laundry festooned on the sheets and stared at the ceiling. All in all, it had been a typical date: arguing for an hour, necking for an hour. *Not exactly how I pictured dating,* he thought. *Certainly not how all those fantasy dates with Buffy went in my head.*

He turned toward the bedside table to stare at the photograph next to his clock radio. Willow's mom had taken that picture of Buffy, Willow, and Xander sophomore year. Buffy's hair was longer then—so, if it came to that, was Xander's.

*Things were simpler then,* he thought. *She was the Slayer, we were the Slayerettes. She killed vampires and demons, and we helped out. Angel was just the mysterious guy who showed up to give cryptic info and disappear, Cordelia was just her usual irritating self, there was no Kendra, no Oz, no Ms. Calendar, no Spike and Drusilla. Just the three of us and Giles against the bad guys. Those were the good times.*

Xander stared at the picture again.

*Yeah, right.*

The fact was, the only reason Xander saw them as the good times was because back then he could delude himself into thinking he had a chance with

Buffy. He still remembered the first time he saw her, the new transfer student walking hesitantly up the stairs to the school grounds. He was so taken with her then that he crashed his skateboard into the stairway railing. Later, he gave her a charm bracelet that said YOURS, ALWAYS. He asked her to the prom. He helped her against the Master and his minions— he even staked one of his best friends after he'd been vamp'd.

*Jesse.* He looked over to the bureau where another, older picture sat: Willow, Jesse, Xander, and Andrea. That was from one of their freshman-year gaming sessions, before Andrea moved away and Jesse got turned into a vampire.

*Who'da thunk it, huh, pal?* he thought at the picture. *Me and Cordelia. Never in a million years would you've believed it.* Xander had known Cordelia since they were both five years old, and it had been hate at first sight. Cordy had said something mean to Willow—he didn't even remember what—and Xander had retaliated in true five-year-old fashion by dumping a bowl of ice cream on her head. She cried, Xander got in trouble, and the tone for their relationship had been set.

Except, of course, for the necking part. That took another twelve years to develop.

The funny thing was, while Willow and Xander had gleefully formed the We Hate Cordelia Chase Fan Club—they even held semiregular meetings— Jesse had always had the hots for her, right up until the moment he died. And now Xander was dating her.

*Well, it could be worse,* he thought. *At least dating Cordelia isn't an immediate threat to my life. My sanity maybe, but not my life.*

Shivering with a chill that had nothing to do with the typically warm Sunnydale night, he remembered a certain substitute biology teacher. . . .

# TEACHER'S PET

## Mid-sophomore Year

# CHAPTER 1

*The vampire's attack caught the kids in the Bronze completely off guard. Even Buffy, the Slayer of vampires, the Chosen One, wasn't ready. She tried to fight the monster, but he was too much for her. A girl screamed as the vampire threw Buffy onto the Bronze's red pool table. Then the undead creature got ready to pounce. Fear showed on the Slayer's face. She was helpless. Would this be the end?*

*Not if I could help it.*

*"May I cut in?" I said as I grabbed the vampire from behind.*

*The vampire tried to go for my throat, but I was ready for him. I slammed his head into the edge of the pool table, stood him up, then gave him a blow to the stomach and a sock to the jaw that sent the creature of the night careening across the room.*

7

*I then went over to the pool table and helped Buffy up. She looked stunning in her low-cut red dress. "Are you all right?" I asked, staring into her deep blue eyes.*

*Those eyes stared back at me with gratitude—and longing. "Thanks to you," she said breathlessly, taking my hand in hers. She looked down and said, "You hurt your hand."*

*I followed her gaze. I hadn't even noticed the pain. After all, there was a job that needed doing. What did a small slicing-open of the skin matter to me?*

*"Will you still be able to—?" Buffy started asking before her voice caught.*

*I completed the question: "Finish my solo and then kiss you like you've never been kissed before?"*

*She nodded, smitten. I smiled. Around me, all the girls in the Bronze seemed to melt. Some shot venomous looks at Buffy, as if to say,* Why her? What did *she* do to deserve *him?*

*Nobody noticed that the vampire was stirring. I did, but pretended not to while I headed back to the stage and my abandoned guitar. As I passed by an overturned table, I yanked off one of its legs, whirled, and threw it unerringly at the now-upright vampire, all in one smooth motion. The makeshift stake found its target. The vampire fell to the ground and crumbled to dust.*

*Buffy clasped her hands over her heart; tears started to form in her eyes. What can I say? I have that effect on women.*

*I leaped back onto the stage, picked up my Fender guitar, and proceeded to whomp out one of the many killer solos in my extensive repertoire.*

*In front of me, Buffy walked up to the base of the stage and said, "You're drooling."*

*Huh?*

"Xander, you've got a little . . ." Buffy Summers said, indicating her chin.

Xander blinked, then wiped at his chin. Sure enough, there had been drool.

On the one hand, he was grateful to Buffy for alerting him to the drool thing before the lights went up in biology class. On the other hand, he really would rather have stayed in his fantasy until Dr. Gregory's even-more-dull-than-one-could-possibly-imagine slideshow ended.

Sitting at the black Formica lab table that he shared with Willow Rosenberg, he tried to figure out what the teacher was talking about.

". . . ancestors were here long before we were. Their progeny will be here long after we are gone."

*Whose progeny?* Xander thought, suddenly panicking. *What is he talking about?* He looked over at Willow, who was, of course, rapt, hanging on Dr. Gregory's every word.

Just as he was about to whisper a question to Willow, the teacher said, "The simple and ubiquitous ant."

*Ah, good. Ants,* Xander thought, relieved. *I know ants. I've been stepping on them since I was a kid.*

Then Dr. Gregory shut the slide projector off and turned on the lights. Suddenly, Xander was grateful that Buffy had brought him back to earth when she did. Another minute, and his drool would have been on display for all the class to see.

Dr. Michael Gregory stared out at his students through his distance glasses as he turned the lights on. As expected, about half the students looked like they had just been awakened from a sound sleep. He enjoyed doing slideshows, not for their educational value, but so he could see who was actually paying attention. Naturally, Rosenberg was completely alert. Just as naturally, her lab partner, Harris, wasn't.

To his disappointment, the pair at the table next to them, Summers and Mall, weren't either.

From Mall, he expected it. A football star, Blayne Mall had brains and decent grades, though not as good as they should have been. He saw sports as his life and school only as a necessary evil.

But from Buffy Summers, the new transfer student, Dr. Gregory had been hoping for more.

Walking down the middle aisle between the two rows of lab tables, he said, "Now, if you read the homework," and he noticed several students squirming at that, "you should know the two ways that ants communicate. Ms. Summers?"

Summers got the deer-in-headlights look that characterized the high school student who had no clue. "Ways that ants communicate . . ." she said, using the classic stall of repeating the question.

Dr. Gregory nodded.

"With *other* ants . . ." she added, extending the stall.

"From the homework," he repeated, "ants are communicating . . ."

Summers was now making eye contact with a point just over his right shoulder. "Uhm, uh, touch—and, um—B.O.?" Obviously, Rosenberg was giving her hints: probably touching and smelling Harris.

Laughter spread throughout the class. Next to her, Mall said, "Thank God someone finally found the courage to mention that."

Ignoring him, Dr. Gregory said, "That would be touch and *smell,* Ms. Summers. Is there anything else Ms. Rosenberg would like to tell you?" The teacher didn't have to turn around to see Rosenberg's patented guilty look.

Then the bell rang. Before it even finished, the sound of stools scraping linoleum could be heard as students got up and prepared to bolt to their next class. "All right, chapters six through eight by tomorrow, people," he called out over the din, then turned back to Summers. "Can I see you for a moment?"

Again, Summers got the deer-in-headlights look.

As the other students filed out, Dr. Gregory noticed Mall calling out to one of the girls walking by in the hall. "Cheryl, wait up, doll."

*"Doll"?* the teacher thought. *Haven't heard anyone use that since I was in high school.*

Mall turned to Harris. "Isn't she something? Do you know what a woman like that wants?" Before Harris had the chance to reply, Mall said, "No, I guess you wouldn't."

As the football player walked off with a grin on his face, Harris called out: "Something really cutting!" Then he turned to Rosenberg. "Sometimes I just go with the generic insult."

Nodding, Rosenberg said, "Why pay more for the brand name?"

Dr. Gregory shook his head. *If they devoted as much time to studying as they did to their witticisms, the whole class would be in the National Honor Society.*

After a few moments, the class was empty, except for Dr. Gregory—who had no class to teach this period—and Summers.

As he gathered up the slides he needed to go through for his next class, he said to her, "I gather you had a few problems at your last school."

"Well, what teenager doesn't?"

"Cut school," he said, checking a couple of the slides to make sure they were the right set, "get in fights, burn down the gymansium?" She seemed surprised that he knew all this, so he added, "Principal Flutie showed me your permanent record."

"Look, that fire," she said, stammering, "I mean, there were *major* extenuating circumstances. Actually, it's kind of funny."

He walked over to the closet to retrieve his reading glasses. "I can't wait to see what you're going to do here—"

"Destructo-girl, that's me," she said ruefully.

"But I suspect it's going to be great."

This time Summers looked confused. "You mean 'great' in a bad way?"

Dr. Gregory smiled as he cleaned off his reading glasses with his tie. "You've got a first-rate mind and you can think on your feet. Imagine what you could accomplish if you actually did the—"

"The homework thing?"

"The homework thing," he repeated. "I understand you probably have a good excuse for not doing it. Amazingly enough, I don't care. I know you can excel in this class and so I expect no less. Is that clear?"

"Yeah," she said. "Sorry."

Students always said they were sorry. Just once, he wanted one to mean it. "Don't be sorry. Be smart. And please don't listen to the principal or anyone else's negative opinion about you. Let's make them eat that permanent record. What do you say?"

Summers smiled a genuine smile, which was exactly what Dr. Gregory was hoping for. "Okay. Thanks," she said.

Dr. Gregory returned the smile. "Chapters six through eight."

Nodding resolutely, Summers left the room.

As he put on his reading glasses and turned his attention back to the slides on his desk, Dr. Gregory thought, *A good reaction. Amazing what a difference it makes when you treat them like human beings.*

He once again turned off the fluorescent overhead lights and switched the lightboard on. The slides were for the advanced-placement, college-level class of seniors tomorrow morning. *No worries about* them *nodding off during the slideshow.*

Peering at the slide, he saw that it was, as expected, from a species of salamander. As a general rule, Michael Gregory preferred reptiles and amphibians. He found their habits much more fascinating. Insects just didn't interest him, and he would be grateful when the sophomores moved on to something else in another two weeks.

A strange noise sounded from behind him. He thought he heard something shuffling.

Then he was grabbed by the neck and yanked from his stool. His reading glasses went flying onto the floor.

The last thing Dr. Gregory saw was what looked like huge mandibles.

His last thought was, *But that's impossible.*

# CHAPTER 2

As a general rule, Buffy Summers thought Sunnydale, California, would be pictured in the dictionary next to the phrase *boring suburb*—if it weren't for the Hellmouth. But aside from the occasional bit of evil, Sunnydale was as dull as dull got.

*Thank God for the Bronze,* she thought. The club catered to underage students, thus providing the only real nightlife for those not old enough to drink legally.

Tonight, they had a good rock band playing, but not of the thrash or metal variety, therefore allowing Buffy to carry on a conversation with Willow without too much shouting.

"So," Willow asked gravely, "how'd it go after bio class?"

"Actually, it went pretty well," Buffy said. "Dr. Gregory didn't chew me out or anything. He was really cool." Sighing, she added, "But Flutie showed him my permanent record. Apparently, I fall somewhere between Charles Manson and a really *bad* person." That had been the one part of her talk with the teacher that annoyed her. When she first arrived at Sunnydale High, Flutie had made noises about how her past record didn't matter and she was starting with a clean slate. *So much for that, if he's showing it to every teacher.*

"And you can't tell Dr. Gregory what really happened at your old school?" Willow asked with a mock-innocent smile.

"I was fighting vampires? I'm thinking he might not believe me," Buffy said dryly.

Willow nodded. "Yeah, he probably gets that excuse all the time."

Buffy smiled. That was one of the things she liked best about Willow. Anyone could be sarcastic, but Willow was the only person she knew who could do it in a nice way.

Their conversation was interrupted by the approach of Cordelia Chase. *Speaking of people who do things in a nice way,* Buffy thought, *here's the world champion of people who don't.*

"Here lies a problem," the brunette cheerleader announced as she came up to Buffy and Willow. "What used to be my table occupied by pitiful losers. Of course, we'll have to burn it."

Buffy gritted her teeth. Cordelia had been the first person to talk to an awkward-feeling transfer student when she arrived at Sunnydale High, but Buffy quickly got on her bad side. Cordelia being the most popular girl in the class, if not the school, meant that now Buffy's chances of expanding her circle of friends beyond Willow and Xander were fairly slim.

*Not that I'm sure I want to expand it to include anyone influenced by her,* she thought. She was also tired of being on the wrong end of Cordelia's insults, and so looking at the well-etched tabletop she said with mock gravity, "Sad. You have so many memories here. You and Lawrence, you and Mark, you and John. You spent the better part of your *J* through *M* here."

Taken aback by an actual response, Cordelia simply made a *tcha* noise and moved on.

"Wow. No comeback," Buffy said, impressed.

"You brought up bad memories," Willow said. "Lawrence dumped her before she had a chance to dump him. It's a sore point."

All in all, Xander liked the Bronze better in his fantasy. For one thing, there were more girls. The only girls present here had one of two drawbacks: they were attached to some guy or they were attached to Cordelia. Already, Her Royal Creepiness was holding court for her subjects at the coffee bar.

Xander wandered up toward the stage, standing in the same spot from which Buffy gazed up at him in his dream. He gave the guitarist/lead singer a quick nod. The singer just looked at him like he was a dead cockroach and then ignored him.

*Next time,* Xander decided, *I'm thinking maybe I should try that with someone I actually know.*

Having already made a moderate fool of himself, he

sought out Buffy and Willow. He wandered over to the couches near the coffee bar, but found only Blayne and one of his fellow football dorks, whose name Xander couldn't remember. If Blayne hadn't been Buffy's lab partner, he probably wouldn't have remembered his name, either. Xander made it a rule not to remember the names of people more athletic than he was.

"Seven," Blayne was saying. At first, Xander assumed they were comparing IQs, but then he added, "Including Cheryl. I tell you though, her sister was looking to make it eight."

"Ooh, Cheryl's sister?" the other jock said, eyes wide. "The one in college?"

"Home for the holidays and looking for love. She's not my type, though. Girl's really gotta have something to go with me."

Without thinking, Xander said, "Something like a lobotomy?"

"Xander," Blayne sneered. "How many times have you scored?"

"Well . . ." Xander said hesitantly. *Why do I get myself into these things?*

"It's just a question," Blayne said with an evil smile.

"Are we talking today or the whole week?" Xander asked, stalling. He was looking frantically around for Buffy and Willow. Finally, he sighted them. "Ooh. Duty calls."

Quickly, he went over to where the two girls were walking. He said, "Babes!" loud enough for Blayne and his crony to hear as he put one arm around each of them.

"What are you doing?" Buffy asked.

"Work with me here," Xander said quickly before Buffy did something unfortunate, like elbow him in the ribs. "Blayne had the nerve to question my manliness. I'm just gonna give him a visual."

Buffy still looked at him like he was nuts, but Willow, bless her, clutched Xander tightly. "We'll show him."

Xander turned and gave Blayne a thumbs-up. Blayne just shook his head. Xander knew this was hitting below the belt. When Buffy first arrived, and had been assigned to be lab partners with Blayne (his previous lab partner had transferred out the week after school began), the hero of the varsity football Razorbacks tried to make time with her. The Slayer came within a hairsbreadth of dislocating his shoulder, and he backed off.

"I don't believe it," Buffy said.

"I know," Xander said. "And after all my conquests—"

Before he could continue, Buffy broke out of the embrace and approached a guy who had just walked into the club. Xander peered into the shadows—the man seemed to be avoiding direct light—and saw a tall, remarkably good-looking young man with short dark hair, wearing all black.

"Who's that?" Xander asked, indignant that Buffy would know someone he didn't.

"That must be Angel," Willow said. "I think."

"That weird guy that warned her about all the vampires?" Shortly after Buffy arrived in Sunnydale, Angel—or "Cryptic Guy," as Buffy had taken to calling him—warned her about the Harvest. Buffy did indeed stop that particular vampire suck-fest, and that was the last she saw of Angel.

However, in all her talk of Cryptic Guy, Buffy had never mentioned what he looked like.

"That's him," Willow said. "I'll bet you."

Even more indignantly, Xander said, "Well, he's buff! She never said anything about him being buff."

"You think he's buff?"

"He's a very attractive man!" Xander cried, then lowered his voice. *Bad enough Blayne's dissing my studliness, the last thing I need is everyone hearing me talk about attractive men.* "How come *that* never came up?"

"Well, look who's here." Buffy said by way of greeting.

"Hi," Angel said, a response that, to Buffy's mind, seemed kind of inadequate.

"I'd say it's nice to see you, but then we both know that's a big fib." *That's right, you don't like this guy,* she told herself firmly. *He's an annoying, mysterious person who won't give a straight answer. You don't like him.*

*So stop staring into those glorious soulful eyes of his. . . .*

"I won't be long," he said.

"No, you'll just give me a cryptic warning about some exciting new catastrophe and then disappear into the night, right?"

He looked down at her with those eyes and said, "You're cold."

"You can take it."

"I mean, you look cold." He removed his jacket and put it around her shoulders.

*Oh God, this feels wonderful.* "Little big on me."

Then she noticed the three long, parallel cuts on his arm. The cuts looked recent. "What happened?" she asked.

"I didn't pay attention."

*There he goes with the cryptic stuff again.* "To somebody with a big fork?" she prompted.

"He's coming."

"The fork guy?" *Why is it so hard for him to give a straight answer? And why does he have to look so gorgeously vulnerable?*

"Don't let him corner you. Don't give him a moment's warning. He'll rip your throat out."

It was quite possibly the longest string of words Angel had put together since she met him. She was, despite herself, impressed. "Okay, I give you improved marks for that one. Ripping the throat out: it's a strong visual, noncryptic."

He almost smiled. He had a very nice almost-smile that made her long to see the full one. "I have to go," he said.

*Of course.* Before she even could say anything, he was gone, melting into the shadows. *God, you'd think he was a vampire or something.*

"Sweet dreams to you, too," she muttered.

Xander watched as the two of them talked for a few minutes, then Angel took off his leather jacket and put it on Buffy.

Xander was outraged. "Oh, *right,* give her your

jacket. It's a balmy night, nobody needs to be trading clothing out there."

"I don't think she even likes him," Willow said hesitantly.

Xander doubted that Willow really believed that any more than he did.

The following morning, Xander wandered the Sunnydale High quad with a spring in his step and a song in his heart. True, he learned last night that Angel looked like some kind of slacker version of a Greek god, but Xander saw no reason to dwell on annoying things out of his control. He had just learned of a good thing out of his control, and he wanted to share it with the world.

Or, at the very least, with Buffy and Willow.

He sighted Willow sitting on one of the brick walls, going over her biology homework, and also Giles and Buffy approaching that same wall. As he got closer, Xander caught the tail end of the conversation between the Slayer and her Watcher, a tall bespectacled Brit in tweed.

"That's all he said?" Giles asked. "'Fork' guy?"

*Aha,* Xander deduced. *Giving the Watcher the 411. Very cool.*

"That's all Cryptic Guy said: fork guy," Buffy said, confirming.

"I think there are too many guys in your life," Giles said with a laugh, then added, "I'll see what I can find out."

They had arrived at the wall where Willow sat just as Xander also reached it. Giles looked up at the sky. "God, every day here is the same."

"Bright, sunny, beautiful—how *ever* can we escape this torment?" Buffy said with a roll of her eyes.

The librarian gave her one of his looks, exchanged good mornings with Xander, then went off to bury himself in the stacks.

Wanting to share his good news, Xander immediately started in on it. "Guess what I just heard in the office? No Dr. Gregory today. Ergo, those of us who blew off our science homework aren't as dumb as we look." He punctuated the statement by closing Willow's bio textbook.

"What happened?" Buffy asked. "Is he sick?"

Xander shrugged. "They didn't say anything about sick—something about missing."

"He's missing?"

Xander frowned. "Well, let me think. The cheerleaders were modeling their new short skirts, I kinda got—" Buffy shot him one of her looks, which, annoyingly, was just like one of Giles's, and Xander grew serious. "Yeah, they said missing. Which is . . . bad?"

"If something's wrong, yeah."

Xander felt like he'd missed something. No bio teacher meant a substitute, which meant, in essence, a free period. What could be wrong?

Willow, as usual, explained: "He's one of the only teachers that doesn't think Buffy is a felon."

Mustering up his sincerity, Xander said, "I'm really sorry. I'm sure he'll—iya huh huh huh!"

He had intended to finish the sentence with the words *turn up,* but he had been distracted by a sight that made every overactive hormone in his body stand at attention.

The woman who walked down one of the quad's pathways was remarkable in many ways. For one thing, she was a woman in a setting primarily populated by girls; for another, she was attractive.

Though *attractive* didn't really seem to cut it.

*The most beautiful woman ever to walk the face of the earth* came closer, but even that seemed insufficient.

She had black hair cropped at her neck, sultry eyes, and the most amazing, pouty lips that Xander had ever seen. They were the kind of lips that simply begged to be kissed. At least, Xander hoped that's what they begged for. She also wore a simple black jacket over a white shirt or blouse or something, and a skirt that wasn't quite a miniskirt, but was sufficiently short to display two of the best legs Xander had ever seen. And she didn't wear pantyhose—Xander had been staring at women's legs long enough to know the difference. Those were her natural legs.

To Xander's amazement and glee, she walked right up to him. "Could you help me?" she asked. Her voice was mellifluous, with just enough of a hint of an accent to sound moderately exotic, but not enough of one to place it.

All thought fled from Xander Harris. His mind was filled solely with this incredible image of beauty before him.

"Uhhh—yes."

"I'm looking for Science One-oh-nine."

"Oh, it's um—" His mind remained blank, but for the image of her. He had no idea where Science 109 was. He wasn't entirely sure he could remember his full name if he were asked to provide it. "I go there every day," he said with a short bark of laughter, then turned to Buffy and Willow in a panic. "Oh God, where is it?"

Before anyone could respond, a voice belonging to the teenager whom Xander right there decided he hated more than anyone else who ever lived said, "Hi. Blayne Mall. I'm going there right now. It's not far from the varsity field where I took all-city last year."

"Oh. Thank you, Blayne," she said, and Blayne led her off. The football star gave Xander a friendly pat on the shoulder as he led the vision of perfection off toward the main building.

"It's funny," he said to the two girls, "how the earth never opens up and swallows you when you want it to."

Buffy and Willow looked completely unsympathetic. In fact, they were smiling.

*Women. Can't rely on 'em.*

"Come on," Buffy said, getting up, "we'll take you to Science One-oh-nine. If you want, you can even drop bread crumbs so you can find your way the next time someone asks you directions."

"Hardy har har," Xander said. Willow also rose from the wall, and the three of them went to bio class.

Xander noticed that the goddess was standing at the front of the class. She had removed the jacket, revealing a white sleeveless shirt or blouse or whatever that exposed a pair of arms that were like porcelain.

She wrote the words *Natalie French* on the blackboard. *So now she has a name. And a function: she's the sub. There is a god.* He had nothing personal against Dr. Gregory—he was as decent a human being as a teacher could possibly be, which put him right above slugs in Xander's pantheon—but he could stay missing forever as far as Xander was concerned.

He heard Willow say, "What's wrong?" Xander turned to see Buffy kneeling down to pick something up off the floor.

That something was a pair of glasses with a cracked lens. "If Dr. Gregory dropped his glasses, why wouldn't he pick them up?" Buffy asked. Shrugging, she put the glasses on one of the tables and took her seat next to the hated Blayne.

The final bell rang, and the class settled down. "My name," said the most glorious voice in the universe, "is Natalie French, and I'll be substituting for Dr. Gregory."

Buffy asked, "Do you know when he's coming back?"

*Who cares?* Xander thought.

"No, I don't, um—" she consulted her seating chart, "Buffy. They just call and tell me where they want me."

Blayne muttered, "I'll tell you where I want you."

"Excuse me, Blayne?"

*Oh sure,* Xander thought, *you don't need to check the chart for him. Just 'cause he walked you to the stupid class . . .*

"I was just wondering if you were gonna pick up where Dr. Gregory left off," Blayne said quickly.

"Yes," Ms. French said with a smile that lit up the entire room. "His notes tell me you were right in the middle of insect life." She went over to the display table and picked up one of the glass cases that had a plastic replica of some kind of bug in it. "The praying mantis is a fascinating creature, forced to live alone. Who can tell me why—Buffy?"

Buffy stared at the case for a moment, then said, "Well, the words *bug ugly* kinda spring to mind."

The smile disappeared, and Ms. French's face darkened. Xander found himself momentarily afraid of her. "There's nothing *ugly* about these unique creatures." Then her face returned to its normal, magnificent self. "The reason they live alone is because they're cannibals."

Several students made *eeeww* noises. Xander was not among them. He was too busy staring.

"It's hardly their fault," Ms. French went on. "It's the way nature designed them: noble, solitary, and prolific. Over eighteen hundred species worldwide, and in nearly all of them, the female is the larger and more aggressive than the male."

Blayne, having apparently forgotten the shoulder incident, leaned over to Buffy. "Nothing wrong with an aggressive female." Buffy shot him a look and he straightened up. Xander couldn't help but smile at that, then went back to staring at Ms. French, who had now picked up a textbook and began reading from it and walking up the aisle.

"The California mantis lays her eggs and then finds a mate to fertilize them. Once he's played his part, she covers the eggs in a protective sac and attaches it to a leaf or a twig out of danger." She held up the textbook and showed it to the class. Xander had no idea what the picture portrayed, as he found himself transfixed by her eyes.

She continued: "Now, if she's done her job correctly, in a few months, she'll have several hundred

27

offspring." She put the textbook down, and looked around the room. Her eye caught something on the bulletin board. "You know, we should make some model egg sacs for the Science Fair. Who would like to help me do that after school?"

Xander's hand shot up. So, he noticed, did Blayne's—and pretty much every other guy in the class.

"Good," she said with another one of her smiles. "I warn you, it's a delicate art. I'd have to work with you very closely—one on one."

*Oh my dear God, I'm in heaven,* Xander thought.

28

# CHAPTER 3

Before Xander knew what was happening, bio class was over. He drifted through the rest of the morning, then found himself at lunch. It was quite likely that things had happened in his other morning classes, but he was hard-pressed to recall any of them. All he could think about was Ms. French—that, and the fact that he got the following night's slot for the one-on-one session with her to make the model egg sacs. Blayne, of course, got tonight's slot, but Xander chalked that up to her being nice because he showed her the way to the classroom.

He met up with Buffy and Willow at the entrance to the cafeteria, and together they went to greet the midday meal with the usual sense of anticipation and dread.

A sign proclaimed the latest culinary disaster from

the graduates of the Sunnydale School of Medieval Torture. Buffy read it aloud. "'Hot dog surprise.' Be still my heart."

"Call me old fashioned," Willow said, "but I don't want any more surprises in my hot dogs."

Xander smiled, picked up a tray, then looked at his reflection in the stainless steel finish of a napkin holder. "I wonder what she sees in me. Probably just the quiet good looks coupled with a certain smoky magnetism." The girls looked at him questioningly. *No,* he thought, *this is the part where you agree with me.* He hated it when they didn't follow the script. "Ms. French," he explained. "You two are probably a little too young to understand what an older woman would see in a younger man."

"Oh, I understand," Buffy said.

"Good," Xander said. *Maybe there's hope for her yet.*

"A younger man is too dumb to wonder why an older woman can't find someone her own age and too desperate to care about the surgical improvements."

"What surgical improvements?" He chose to ignore the rest of Buffy's diatribe, fobbing it off as a jealous tiff.

"Well," Willow said to Buffy, "he *is* young."

"And so terribly innocent," Buffy added.

With that, the two girls went off to fetch drinks. Xander called after them. "Hey, those that can, do. Those that can't—laugh at those who can do." *Well, that wallowed in lameness. If I keep this up, I'll lose my membership in the Witty Rejoinder Club.*

Before he could come up with anything better,

Blayne went by, his tray piled high with inedible delights. "Gotta carb up for my one on one with Ms. French today. When's yours? Oh right, tomorrow. You came in second, I came in first. I guess that's what they call natural selection."

Xander was really starting to hate Blayne's habit of answering his own questions. "I guess that's what they call rehearsal."

Blayne wandered off, unable to muster up a comeback. *Much better,* Xander thought. *Rejoinder Boy strikes.*

"Excuse you," said an obnoxious voice. Xander looked up to see Cordelia shoving her way past Buffy with her usual absence of decorum. She plowed forward into the kitchen, stood in front of one of the huge fridges, and held up a slip of paper like a cop holding a badge. "Medically prescribed lunch. My doctor ships it daily. I'll only be here as long as I can hold my breath."

Xander shook his head. This was Cordy's latest diet, which included specific food from the latest in a series of dieticians—at least, according to two of her friends, who had discussed it at great length during the previous day's English class. Cordelia had many flaws, but the need to diet had never struck Xander as one of them.

Before he could turn away and go back to thinking about Ms. French, he heard an ear-piercing wail from the kitchen.

It was Cordelia, who stood in abject terror before the now-open fridge. Buffy exchanged a glance with Willow, then they both ran into the kitchen. Xander followed about three steps behind them.

The minute he arrived behind Buffy and Willow, Xander was sorry he did so.

Hanging in the fridge like it was a massive side of beef was a human body.

The body wore a lab coat with the words *Dr. Gregory* sewn on the chest.

The head was missing.

"His head! His head!" Cordy cried. "Ohmigod, where's his *head?*"

Much later—after the police had been called, the body taken away, and statements given—Xander joined Willow and Buffy in the library. The girls looked stunned, and Xander felt much the same way. Even Giles, who usually radiated calmness in the worst of situations, seemed a little off.

"Here," Giles said to Buffy, handing her a glass of water. "Drink this."

"No, thank you," Buffy said as she took the glass and drank from it.

"I've never seen—" Xander started, stopped, then tried again. "I mean, I've never seen anything like—" Again, his mouth wouldn't work properly. Finally, he said, "That was *new.*"

"Who would want to hurt Dr. Gregory?" Willow asked.

Giles shook his head. "He didn't have any enemies on the staff that I'm aware of. He was a civilized man. I liked him."

"So did I," Buffy said in an unusually small voice.

*Sure, make me feel worse,* Xander thought. All he could think about was that he had wished Dr. Gregory would stay missing forever. This wasn't what he had in mind.

"Well, we're gonna find out who did this," Willow said with determination. "We'll find them, then we'll stop them."

"Count on it," Buffy said with a good deal more determination.

"What do we know?" Giles asked.

"Not a lot," Buffy said. She stood up and started pacing. "He was killed on campus. I'm guessing, the last day we saw him."

Giles frowned. "How did you work that out?"

"He didn't change his clothing."

Xander spoke up. "This is a question that no one particularly wants to hear, but—where did they put his head?"

"Good point," said Willow. "I *didn't* want to hear that."

"Angel," Buffy said suddenly.

*What does he have to do with this?* Xander thought angrily.

"He warned me that something was coming," she continued.

*Oh, okay. Mystery-guy stuff. That's okay, then.*

Giles nodded. "Yes. Yes, he did, didn't he? And I wish I knew what he meant." He wandered over to the table to pick up one of his seemingly infinite supply of musty reference tomes. "I've been trying to gather more information about the Master, our local vampire king. There was one oblique reference to a vampire who displeased the Master and cut his hand off in penance."

"Cut off his hand and replaced it with a fork?" Buffy asked.

Giles shrugged. "I don't know what he replaced it with."

Xander didn't get it. "So why would he come after a teacher?"

"I'm not certain he did," Giles said. "There was an incident two nights ago involving a homeless person in Weatherly Park. He was practically shredded. But nothing like Dr. Gregory."

Buffy said, succinctly, "Fork guy doesn't do heads."

"Not historically."

"And," she added, "Dr. Gregory's blood wasn't drained."

*Thanks for the reminder, Buff,* Xander thought, remembering the significant amount of blood in the fridge. At first, he'd tried to convince himself that it came from the meat that was usually stored there, but even Xander's tremendous capacity for self-delusion didn't go that far.

Aloud, he said, "So there's something *else* out there? Besides Silverware Man? Oh, this is fun. We're on Monster Island."

"We're on a Hellmouth," Buffy reminded him. "The center of mystical convergence." Giles shot her a look, and she added, contritely, "I guess it's the same thing."

"Yes," Giles said, "unpleasant things do gravitate here, it's true, but we don't know there's anything besides this chap. He's still our likely suspect."

"Where was that guy killed," Buffy asked, "Weatherly Park?"

"Buffy," Giles said, "I know you're upset, but this

is no time to go hunting. Not until we know more. Please, promise me you won't do anything rash."

"Cross my heart," Buffy said sincerely.

Despite the situation, Xander almost laughed. He knew Buffy would be making a beeline for Weatherly Park the minute it got dark.

The minute it got dark, Buffy put on the jacket Angel had given her *(and why did he have to do something so nice and adorable and sweet?)* and made a beeline for Weatherly Park. The park wasn't terrifically large as parks went. Willow had told her a bit about it when she and Xander brought her here one recent weekend. It was originally the site of Weatherly Mansion, home of the then-richest family in Sunnydale. In 1969, Augustus "Gussie" Weatherly went completely nuts and was put away. Buffy had always meant to ask Giles if Gussie's going cuckoo was Hellmouth-related.

After he died in a loony bin six years later, Gussie's heirs—who all lived in New York—sold the land to the City of Sunnydale to make into a park. Originally, it had been isolated on the outskirts of town, but now it was surrounded by houses.

More recently, a fence had been erected around the park's perimeter. Willow had said it was to keep the homeless out when the park was closed at night. *Not doing a very good job, if they're still getting mauled in here,* Buffy thought as she hopped over that fence.

It was a quiet night with no breeze. *Quiet like a tomb,* she thought, then put that image out of her head. *I think about tombs way too much for a sixteen year old.* Still, the quiet meant that she was guaranteed to hear anything unusual—like fork guy.

"Shouldn't be out here at night, li'l lady," said a slurred voice so suddenly that Buffy nearly jumped out of her skin. She whirled to see a homeless man shambling along. He wore a coat that was way too warm for SoCal and carried a bottle in a bag.

*Nice work, Slayer,* she thought, annoyed at herself. *Should've heard him coming.* A whiff of something like rotted peaches wafted to her nostrils. *Should've smelled him coming, too.*

"S'dangerous," the guy continued, then wandered off in whatever direction the bottle told him to take.

Turning a corner, Buffy found what looked like a body on the ground—another homeless guy, as inappropriately dressed as the last. He looked dead.

But after a second, he started snoring.

As a breeze rustled a nearby bush, she wondered what her next move should be.

She moved toward the bush before she even had the conscious thought: *there's no breeze to rustle that bush.* Something was moving in there.

Moving to push the branches out of the way, she realized that the plant wasn't rooted. It had been placed there to cover a storm drain.

*Three guesses on who put it there,* she thought. *And your first hint is, he's a big fan of* A Farewell to Arms.

Then the vampire leaped at her.

At first glance, he looked like an ordinary vampire. He had the fangs, the sloped forehead, the lack of eyebrows, the hooded eyes. His hair was longer than the well-dressed vamp usually kept it these days, but Buffy wasn't about to quibble.

What made him really stand out from the crowd

were the six-inch-long, razor-sharp claws where his right hand used to be.

The six-inch-long, razor-sharp claws that were moving toward Buffy's head . . .

She ducked his swipe. He had lunged, so his back was now exposed. Buffy took advantage of this to land two kicks to his lower spinal region before he could take another shot. Again, she ducked; again, she got two kicks in, then added a punch to the jaw for good measure.

He took a third swipe. *Let's not get too repetitive,* Buffy thought. Claw guy was a one-trick vamp. This time she grabbed his arm, and used the momentum of his swipe to flip him in a classic *aikido* maneuver.

As he landed with a thud on his back, Buffy took out a stake and prepared to finish him off.

Unfortunately, he quickly rolled out of the way and started to get up. Buffy knocked him down with another kick, and then—

"Hold it! Police!"

*Oh, great.*

Several cops were coming over a hill—led by, of all people, the first homeless guy. *No wonder he warned me,* Buffy realized. *They were trying to nail their murderer and had someone undercover as Homeless Harry. Well, sorry, guys, but you're way out of your depth on this one.*

Claw guy took advantage of Buffy's momentary distraction to bolt into the underbrush.

"I heard him—spread out!" yelled one of the cops.

Muttering a curse, Buffy chased after him.

She made it to the fence just as claw guy finished

climbing it to the other side. He was going after a woman walking on the sidewalk, carrying a bag of groceries in each hand.

Buffy was about to call out a warning and vault the fence when she saw something that stunned her.

The woman turned around. It was Ms. French, the bio sub.

She stared right at claw guy.

Claw guy backed off.

*No, he's not just backing off,* Buffy realized. *He's terrified.* In her time as the Slayer, Buffy had never seen a vampire so scared when direct sunlight wasn't involved.

Looking for all the world like a cat with his tail between his legs, claw guy scampered to a drain cover, threw it aside, and escaped into the sewer system.

Ms. French—whose facial expression hadn't changed—turned and continued calmly walking down the street as if nothing had happened.

# CHAPTER 4

*Okay,* Buffy thought as she walked into the library the next morning shortly before her bio class, *the first thing Giles is going to do is berate me for going hunting last night—*

"You went hunting last night."

*Two points for the Chosen One.* "Yep," she said.

Giles wasn't finished. "When you promised me you wouldn't."

"Yeah. I lied. I'm a bad person. Let's move on."

"Did you see someone with a fork?" Giles asked a bit tartly.

"More like a jumbo claw."

Giles, who clearly hadn't expected the answer to be *yes,* shot her a look. "Oh," he said. "Well, at least you're not hurt."

"And," she continued, "I saw something else,

39

something much more interesting than your average, run-of-the-mill killer vampire."

"Oh?"

"You know Ms. French, the teacher who's subbing for Dr. Gregory?"

At the mention of the sub's name, Giles did something Buffy had never seen her Watcher do before. It was a sight that was as scary as any she'd ever seen.

He grinned.

"Yes, yes, she's lovely," he said, goofily. Buffy hadn't thought Giles was even capable of goofiness. Quickly, he added, "In a common, extremely well-proportioned way."

*Nice save,* she thought. "Well, I'm chasing claw guy last night, and Ms. Well-Proportioned is heading home. The claw guy takes one look at her and runs screaming for cover."

Giles blinked. "He what? Ran away?"

"He was petrified."

"Of Ms. French?"

"Uh-huh. So," Buffy said, "I'm an undead monster that can shave with my hand. How many things am I afraid of?"

"Not many," Giles said, "and not substitute teachers, as a rule."

"So what's her deal?"

"I think perhaps it would be a good idea if we kept an eye on her."

"Then I'd better get to class," Buffy said, turning and heading for the door. She had less than a minute before the second bell would ring.

As she dashed through the hall, she was intercepted by Principal Flutie. The pudgy, black-haired man was wearing a suit with the latest in a series of hideous ties that would've made great ads for awful Father's Day presents. "You were there, you saw Dr. Gregory, didn't you?" he asked without preamble.

Since Flutie had been standing right there—mostly whining—while Buffy, Cordelia, Willow, Xander, and the kitchen staff all gave their statements to the police, this struck Buffy as an odd question. "You mean yesterday in the cafeteria, when we found him—"

"Don't say dead," Flutie interrupted. "Or decapitated. Or decomposing. I would stay away from *D* words altogether. But you witnessed the event, so this way please," he said, indicating the opposite direction from Science 109.

"Well, no, I'm gonna be late for biology."

"Extremely late," Flutie agreed, leading her down the hallway. "You have to see a counselor. Everyone who saw the body has to see a crisis counselor."

If Buffy saw a crisis counselor every time she came across a dead body, the counselor would have to move into her house. "I really don't need—"

"We all need help with our feelings," Flutie babbled on, "otherwise we bottle them up and before you know it, powerful laxatives are involved. I really believe that if we all reach out to one another, we can beat this thing. I'm always here if you need a hug—but not a real hug, because there's no touching in this school, we're sensitive to wrong touching."

He led her to a bench outside what was usually the school nurse's office, which Buffy refused to sit on. From inside, she could hear someone's voice droning on.

"But I really *really*—"

"No," Flutie interrupted again. "You have to talk to a counselor and start the healing. You have to heal."

"But Mr. Flutie, I—"

"Heal!" he barked, pointing to the bench.

Defeated, Buffy sank into the seat.

*Just my luck, I'm stuck with the touchy-feely principal. Well, feely, anyhow, since we're so "sensitive to wrong touching."*

Buffy leaned back and hoped that Willow would notice if Ms. French did anything weird. Normally, she'd include Xander in that, but he was obviously besotted.

*"Besotted"? I've been hanging around Giles way too long.*

She finally noticed that the droning voice belonged to Cordelia.

"I don't know what to say," she was saying, which was obviously not true. "It was really . . . I mean, one minute, you're in your normal life, and then, 'who's in the fridge?' It really gets to you, a thing like that. It was—let's just say I haven't been able to eat a thing since yesterday. I think I lost like seven-and-a-half ounces—way swifter than the so-called diet that quack put me on. Oh," she added quickly, "I'm not saying that we should kill a teacher every day just so I can lose weight, I'm just saying, when tragedy strikes, you have to look on the bright side. You know, like how even a used Mercedes still has leather seats."

*Okay,* Buffy thought, *it's official. I'm in hell.*

Cordelia finally tired of hearing herself talk and exited. Upon seeing Buffy, she said, "You'll probably need a couple of hours in there. I mean hey, why turn down the free therapy, right?"

Buffy ignored her and went in. She answered all the counselor's questions—*is it my imagination, or is he relieved to get a word in edgewise?*—with simple answers. She had gone through this at Hemery High after she burned down the gymnasium, right before they decided to kick her out. It was impossible for the counselor to do her any good because she couldn't give the counselor the real reason for any of her problems. So she kept her answers simple and was out of there in five minutes.

She ran to bio class only to see that the students were all hunched over tests. "Oh great," she muttered. "A pop quiz."

Two things grabbed her attention immediately after that. One was that her lab table was completely empty. Blayne also missed class.

The other was that Ms. French was standing with her back to the door.

This, in and of itself, wasn't unusual, but she turned her head around to look toward Buffy.

All the way around. Without pivoting the rest of her body at all.

At the last second, Buffy moved from out of sight of the bio class door.

*This,* she decided, *is just too weird.*


After school, she caught Willow up on her day, ending with Ms. French's little neck trick.

Willow was, perhaps understandably, having problems with the concept. "She craned her neck?"

"No, I'm not saying she craned her neck," Buffy

said, exasperated as they entered the library. "We are talking full-on *Exorcist* twist."

"Ouch."

"Which reminds me," Buffy said, remembering the other odd thing in class, "how come Blayne—who worked with her 'one on one' yesterday—isn't here today?"

"Inquiring minds want to know," Willow said, and immediately went for the computer.

Buffy went to Giles, who sat at the main desk, poring over a book. "Any luck?"

"Um, I've not found any creature as yet that strikes terror in a vampire's heart."

"Try looking under 'Things that Can Turn Their Heads All the Way Around.' "

"Nothing human can do that," Giles said.

"No, nothing human." Buffy then had a thought, as parts of chapters six through eight came back to her. "But there are some insects that can. Whatever she is, I'm gonna be ready for her."

With that, she went up the stairs to the stacks.

"What are you going to do?" Giles asked.

Grinning, Buffy said, "My homework." And she went into the stacks.

After wandering around for several seconds, she came back out. "Where are the books on bugs?" she asked Giles.

*The moment has come,* Xander thought triumphantly. He barely slept the night before, and when he did, he dreamed of her. Bio class couldn't come soon enough. When it did, the pop quiz was like a bucket of ice water in the face. Still, he soldiered through it. He was heartened by the fact that Blayne never turned up. *Probably got worn out by a real woman. Well, we Harrises are made of sterner stuff.*

The test was something of a challenge, especially since Xander had barely cracked the bio textbook all year, and then mainly to draw moustaches on the pictures of cells.

But it was worth it for one moment.

*"Keep your eyes straight ahead,"* Ms. French had said, *"on your own test."* Then she walked up behind Xander and put a hand on his shoulder. His heart stopped. In a whisper that he doubted even Willow heard, she said, *"I think you meant 'pollination' for number fourteen."* He gave her a grateful look and changed the answer. She added, *"I'll see you here after school."*

He didn't breathe slowly for the rest of the day.

Now he was set for the one on one.

He walked in as the sub was preparing a sandwich of some kind. "Hi!" he said, grateful that he could manage one-syllable words, at least, in her presence.

"Oh, hi. I was just grabbing a snack. Can I get you something?"

Several answers came to mind, but Xander simply said, "No, thanks, I never eat when I'm making egg sacs." He looked down at a model she had already made. "Wow, if these were real, the bugs'd be—"

"Big as you," she finished.

"Yeah. So," he said, not wanting to dwell on that mental image, "where do we start?"

"Oh, Xander, I've done something really stupid. I hope you can forgive me."

She could have told him that she was responsible

for starting a world war and he would have forgiven her. "Oh, Forgiveness is my middle name. Actually it's LaVelle, and I'd appreciate it if you'd guard that secret with your life."

Xander realized this had to be true love. He'd never told anyone his middle name before. Not even Willow or Jesse or Buffy.

"I have a teacher's conference in half an hour and I left the paint and the papier mâché at home. I don't suppose you'd like to come to my place tonight to work on it there?"

"Come to, uh—your place?"

Up until this point, Xander's love life had primarily consisted of girls laughing hysterically at him when he expressed any kind of romantic interest in them. So to have the most perfect woman in the world invite him to her place at night came as something of a shock.

A good shock, of course, but a shock, nonetheless.

"It'd just be the two of us," she said, adding to both the shock and the joy. "I'd feel more comfortable there, you know, about letting my hair down."

"Right, that's important," he stammered, "'cause when you hair's not down, it's—up." *We're wallowing in lameness again.*

*Oh, who cares? She's invited me to her house.*

"It's a date, then," she said, rooting around the desk for a piece of paper. "Seven-thirty," she added, handing him the paper. "Here's my address. I'll see you tonight."

*She said "date."*

Slowly, not trusting himself to walk steadily without major mental effort, Xander turned and left Science 109.

As soon as the door closed behind him, he threw out his arms and cried, "Ooh, *yes!*"

Buffy came running out to the railing that looked out over the main part of the library. She held a text on praying mantises in her hands. "Dig this," she said excitedly. " 'The praying mantis can rotate its head a hundred and eighty degrees while waiting for its next meal to walk by.' Hah!" she finished, closing the book with a flourish.

When Giles and Willow refused to react, Buffy said, "Well, c'mon guys. Hah?"

Willow brushed her brown hair behind her ear the way she did when she was about to say something she figured people didn't want to hear. "Well, Ms. French is sort of big. For a bug," she added helpfully.

"She is, by and large, woman shaped," Giles added.

Buffy would not be defeated. As she walked down the stairs, she ticked off factoids. "Okay, factoid one: only the praying mantis can rotate its head like that. Factoid two: a pretty whacked-out vampire is scared to death of her. Factoid three: her fashion sense *screams* predator."

That seemed to convince Willow. "The shoulder pads."

"Exactly," Buffy said, triumphantly.

Giles started fiddling with his pen. "If you're right, she'd have to be a shapeshifter, or perception distorter. Well, now, half a mo'," he said, looking like a light bulb went off over his head. "I had a chum at Oxford, Carlyle, with advanced degrees in entomology and mythology."

"Entoma-who?" Buffy asked.

"Bugs and fairy tales," Giles translated dryly.

Buffy nodded. "I knew that," she lied.

"If I recall correctly, poor old Carlyle—just before he went mad—claimed there was some beast—"

Willow interrupted. "Buffy, nine-one-one! Blayne's mom called the school. He never came home last night."

As Buffy walked around the table to join Willow at the computer, Giles asked, "The boy who worked with Ms. French yesterday?"

"Yeah," Willow said. "If Ms. French is responsible for—Xander's supposed to be helping her right now. He's got a crush on a giant insect!"

Willow sounded frantic. Quickly, Buffy said, "Okay, don't panic. I'll warn him. But I need you to hack into the coroner's office for me."

"What are we looking for?" Willow asked.

Buffy suppressed a smile. Willow had a crush of her own: on Xander. Her feelings were patently obvious to everyone except Xander himself, whose obliviousness would have been cute if it didn't hurt Willow so much.

Still, right now Buffy needed Willow to be focused, not worried. Distracting her with some computer nerdity was just the thing to keep her mind off Xander.

"Autopsy on Dr. Gregory. I've been trying to figure out these marks I saw on his corpse. I'm thinking they were teeth." She pointed to a picture in the mantis book. "And these cuddlies should definitely be brushing after every meal." She turned back to Giles. "And you were saying something about a beast?"

Giles had his faraway look on. "Oh, uh, yes, I just need to make one transatlantic telephone call." He headed for his office, then stopped and turned around. "This computer invasion that Willow's performing on the coroner's office—one assumes it is entirely legal?"

"Of course," Buffy said with all the sincerity she could cram into two words.

"Entirely," Willow said at the same time.

Giles obviously didn't buy it for a second. "Right," he said. "Wasn't here, didn't see it, couldn't have stopped you."

"Good idea," Buffy said with more sincere sincerity.

As the librarian disappeared into his office, Buffy grabbed her new leather jacket *(Angel . . . )* and went off in search of Xander, leaving Willow to her hack work.

It took several minutes to find him. He wasn't in the bio classroom, nor the student lounge or cafeteria, and he obviously wasn't in the library, which exhausted his usual haunts. She checked outside, finally finding him walking near the quad.

"Hey," she said as she caught up to him.

He said, "Hey," back.

"So how'd it go with Ms. French?"

Xander shrugged. "Well, it's a bit demanding being her absolute favorite guy in the universe, but I'll muddle through."

*Oh great, he's completely bereft of anything like a clue.* "Xander," she said, "she's not what she seems."

"I know," he said dreamily, "she's so much more."

*Arrrrrgh.* "Okay, um, I'm gonna have to tell you something about her," she said slowly, "and I'm gonna need you to *really* listen, okay?"

"Okay," Xander said, sounding like he meant it.

*Here goes.* "I don't think she's human."

Xander smirked. "I see. So, she's not human, she's . . . ?"

"Technically, a big bug." As Xander's smirk grew into a grin, Buffy added quickly, "This sounds really weird, I'm aware, but—"

"It doesn't sound weird at all," Xander said in the most condescending voice she'd ever heard him use. "I completely understand. I've met someone, and you're jealous."

Buffy gathered every bit of willpower she possessed and did *not* break Xander's neck. "What?"

"Look, there's nothing I could do about it. There's just a certain chemical thing between Ms. French and me."

"I know, I read all about it. It's called, uh, a pheromone. It's a chemical attractant insects give off."

"She's not an insect, she's a woman, okay?" Now Xander sounded exasperated. "Hard as it may be for you to conceive, an actual woman finds me attractive. I realize it's no mystery guy handing out leather jackets. And while we're on the subject, what kind of a girly-name is Angel anyway?"

"What does that have to do with—"

"Nothing," Xander said. "It just kinda bugs me."

Buffy looked into her friend's eyes and saw that there would be no convincing him. He hadn't paid attention to a thing she said, hadn't considered the possibility that she might be right. That was so wildly out of character—and, at the same time, completely in character under the circumstances—that Buffy knew it would be pointless to keep arguing.

"I really gotta . . ." Xander trailed off and left.

Sighing to herself, Buffy headed back to the library. *We've got to find a way to stop her before Xander does something stupid.* She thought a moment, then amended the thought: *stupider.*

# CHAPTER 5

Xander had thought he would never see a sight as glorious as Natalie French when he first saw her walking down the quad.

He was wrong.

That honor had to go to Natalie French when she answered the door the night of his one-on-one egg sac–making session.

She wore—well, not a lot, really. It was a one-piece black dress, cut high on the leg and cut *very* low on the neck.

"Hi," she said with that light-up-the-room smile, "come on in." He entered slowly, his eyes transfixed on the dress's plunging neckline. "Should I change?" she asked. "Is this too—?"

"No, no," Xander said quickly, wanting to get any idea of her changing out of her head as fast as possible. "It's the most beautiful chest—*dress* I've ever seen." *Oh, good one there, Freudian Slip Boy.*

"Thank you, that's sweet." She picked up a pair of long-stemmed glasses and offered him one. "Martini?"

He hesitated. Many guys his age drank at least beer at parties, but Xander didn't get invited to those kinds of parties—mainly because he generally didn't get invited to parties, period. His experiences with alcohol were limited to the occasional glass of wine with dinner at his grandmother's house. *"It's only a little,"* she'd say, *"it won't hurt him."*

"Oh, I'm sorry," she said, noticing his hesitation. "Would you like something else?"

Xander quickly took the glass and sat on one end of the small, but very comfortable couch. She sat on the other end.

"I just need to relax a little," she said. "I'm kind of nervous around you. You're probably cool as a cucumber."

"I like cucumbers. Like in that Greek salad thing with the yogurt. You like Greek food? I'm exempting schwarma, of course. What is that all about, big meat hive?" *Good God, Harris, stop before you make an even bigger fool of yourself.* He drained the martini in one gulp.

A strange fuzzy feeling formed in the base of his throat, leaped around throughout his body for several seconds, then finally settled down in his head.

"Hel-*lo.*"

Ms. French smiled and clinked his empty glass in a toast. "Cheers." She took a sip of her martini—*Oh, okay, you're supposed to sip it. Duh*—then said, "Can

I ask you a personal question?" She slid closer to him. "Have you ever been with a woman before?"

"You mean, like, in the same room?" Xander said, stalling.

"You know what I mean."

"Oh, that. Well, let me think, um, yeah, there was—several. I mean, and uh, quite a few times—and then there was—she was incredibly—" *Give it up.* "No, nuh-uh."

"I know," she said, stroking his hair with her lovely hand. "I can tell."

"You can?" Xander didn't really want to know that his lack of experience was tattooed on his forehead.

"Oh, I *like* it," she said. "You might say . . . I need it."

"Well, needs should, you know—needs should definitely be met as long as they don't require ointments the next day or—"

Xander cut himself off. He could've sworn he heard someone screaming in the distance. "Do you hear—?"

"No."

"Sounds like someone crying—"

"I don't hear anything." She grabbed his hands. Xander swallowed, as he realized that she grabbed them in the exact same way Buffy did in his fantasy during bio class two days earlier. "Your hands are so—hot," Ms. French said.

But Xander's ever-more-muddled brain found itself thinking about the Slayer. "Buffy," he said dreamily. "I love Buffy." He looked at his glass with foggy vision. "Wow. So that's a martini, huh?"

"M-hm," she said, still caressing his hand.

Again Xander heard the yelling, and this time it sounded distinctly like the words, *Somebody help me.*

"Do you hear—"

"Would you like to touch me with those hands?" Ms. French asked.

Five minutes earlier, Xander would have said he wanted nothing more in the world, but now he couldn't get his thoughts to come into focus. He looked down at Ms. French's hands, still stroking his, and tried to concentrate on them. "Your hands are really—serrated?" Suddenly, they weren't human hands anymore, but some kind of—what? Not human, whatever they were.

Then the hand-that-wasn't-a-hand became blurry and indistinct. "That martini—I really think I—"

And then he passed out.

Giles had said he had to make one transatlantic phone call, but he actually made several. According to Willow, he was on his fourth call by the time Buffy returned from her abortive attempt to talk to Xander. Apprently, this Carlyle guy had been transferred to a different loony bin. Night had fallen by the time Giles found the right one.

"Frankly, madam," came the Watcher's voice from his office, "I haven't the faintest idea *what* time it is, nor do I care. Now unlock his cell, unstrap him, and bring him to the telephone immediately, this is a matter of life and death!"

Buffy, having been on the receiving end of Giles's ire once or twice herself, didn't envy the woman on the other end of the line.

"Got it," Willow said. Buffy joined her at the

computer. "Coroner's report, complete with"—she made a face—"yuck, color pictures."

Willow backed away from the monitor, but Buffy leaned in closer. Being the Slayer made her extremely difficult to gross out. In fact, she preferred the more controlled carnage of a medical examiner's report. Vampires tended to be a lot messier when they slashed up a body. This was all neat and orderly.

*Well, except for the lack of a head. They never did find that.*

She compared the marks on what was left of Dr. Gregory's neck to those in the textbook. "They *are* teeth marks," she said triumphantly, "which match perfectly the one insect that nips off its prey's head."

"Okay," Willow said, "I don't like this."

"It's the way they feed: head first. Also, the way they mate. The female bites off the male's head while they're—"

"No, no, no!" Willow said, and Buffy belatedly realized that she perhaps shouldn't have gotten so graphic. "See, Xander is—I like his head, that's where you find his eyes and his hair, and his adorable smile . . ."

"Whoa, take it easy, Will," Buffy said, putting her hand on her friend's shoulder. "Xander is not in any immediate danger. I saw him leave school—he's probably safe at home right now."

Xander awakened to find himself surrounded by—straw? He also no longer sat on Ms. French's couch, but was on a solid, uncomfortable floor in a very dark room. *And,* he realized, *in a cage.*

He looked up to see a giant praying mantis.

*But that's impossible,* he thought.

Then he remembered Buffy's words. *"Technically, a big bug."*

*Oh boy.*

"Ms.—French?" he ventured.

"Please," said the giant praying mantis in the voice he had fallen in love with, "call me Natalie."

*Oh boy.*

Suddenly, a hand grabbed his arm. "Yaaaah!" he cried.

The hand was attached to an arm, which was, in turn, attached to someone in the next cage over. That someone turned out to be: "Blayne?"

Several things were starting to make a sick sort of sense to Xander Harris, primary among them that he was the biggest idiot who ever walked the face of the earth.

"Oh God, oh God, oh God . . ." Blayne was muttering.

"Are you okay?"

"You gotta get me outta here, you gotta—she—she—she gets you and—"

Curiosity warred with revulsion and won. "What? What does she do?"

"Oh God, oh no . . ."

Now that curiosity had won, Xander damn well wanted it satisfied. He reached between the bars and grabbed Blayne by his now-filthy shirt. "Blayne, *what does she do?*"

"She—she takes you out of the cage and she ties you up. Then she, like, starts moving and throbbing and these eggs come shooting out of her—and then—"

"What? Then what?"

"She mates with you."

*A dream come true under other circumstances,* Xander thought. "She—"

"That's not the worst part," Blayne said, now on a roll.

"It's not?"

"Have you seen her teeth? Right while she's—right in the middle of—I saw her do it!" He pointed at a body in the next cage over from Blayne's. Like Dr. Gregory's, it was without benefit of a head. "I don't want to die like that!"

"Blayne, Blayne, chill. It's gonna be okay, we're gonna get out of this."

"You have a plan?" Blayne asked plaintively. "What is it?"

Reluctant as he was to admit to not being in a superior position to the football jock, Xander lamely said, "Just let me perfect it."

Blayne didn't buy it. "Oh God."

Xander sighed, then decided to try actually forming a plan. *Okay, what would Buffy do?* He thought a moment, then: *She'd bend the bars with her super Slayer strength. Fat lotta good that does me.*

Then he looked at the bars to the cage. The metal looked worn in spots. *Maybe, just maybe . . .*

He pulled at one particularly weak-looking bar for several minutes. Beyond, the giant bug formerly known as Ms. French shuffled around doing whatever it was insects did before mating. *Probably doing up her compound eyes just right,* Xander thought as he pulled.

Blayne took time away from saying, "Oh God" a lot

to finally take notice. "What are you—? Don't do anything that'll make her mad."

Xander ignored Blayne, and finally managed to yank one bar loose.

"Hey, all right," Blayne said, brightening. "Now I can get out of my cage—into yours." He frowned. "What'd you do that for?"

Xander held up the bar. "A weapon."

Blayne looked over at the bug. "I think you're gonna need it."

Hiding the bar behind his back, Xander turned to see the bug—*That's right, keep thinking of it as the bug, not Ms. French*—ambling toward them. She stopped in front of Blayne's cage. The pride of the Razorbacks whimpered like a little girl and clambered through the new hole into Xander's cage.

"He did that! He broke the cage! Take him, not me, take him!"

*Way to handle the pressure there, Blayne.*

The bug then went over to Xander's cage, where both boys now sat, and pointed at Blayne with her foreleg. Then she pointed at Xander.

Then she pointed at Blayne again.

"What's she doing?" Xander asked.

"I think it's eenie, meenie, mynie—"

The foreleg settled on Xander.

Swallowing, Xander finished, "—moe."

Rupert Giles hadn't heard Ferris Carlyle's voice in twenty years, and it appeared that the intervening two decades hadn't done much for the old boy's stability.

"I understand, Carlyle. . . . Yes, I'll take every precaution. . . . Absolutely, it sounds exactly like the creature you described. You were right all along, about everything. . . . Well, no, you weren't right about your mother coming back as a Pekingese, but . . . Try to rest, old man. . . . Yes. . . . Ta. . . . 'Bye now."

He hung up the phone with the sensation of having gone crawling in some very unpleasant holes. The old days in Oxford—and afterward—were not memories he chose to revisit often.

Rubbing his left arm briefly, as though it pained him, he rose and went back into the main part of the library, where Buffy and Willow were waiting.

"So now can you tell us about this beast thing?" Buffy asked.

Giles nodded. "Dr. Ferris Carlyle," he said, "spent years transcribing a lost, pre-Germanic language. What he discovered he kept to himself—until several teenage boys were murdered in the Cotswolds. Then he went hunting for it."

" 'It' being—?"

"He calls her a She-Mantis. This type of creature, the Kleptes-Virgo, or virgin thief, appears in many cultures: the Greek Sirens, the Celtic sea-maidens who tore the living flesh from the bones of—"

"Giles," Buffy interrupted, "while we're young."

Sighing, Giles reminded himself yet again of this Slayer's almost nonexistent attention span. "Well, basically, the She-Mantis assumes the form of a beautiful woman and then lures innocent virgins back to her nest."

"Virgins? Well, Xander's not a . . . I mean, he's probably—"

"Gonna die!" Willow finished as she got up and ran to the phone.

"Okay, okay," Buffy said covering the awkward pause, "so this thing is breeding. And we have to find it and snuff it. Any tips on the snuffing part?"

"Carlyle recommends cleaving all body parts with a sharp blade."

"Slice and dice," Buffy said.

Resisting the urge to say, *I believe that's what I said,* Giles instead added, "Whatever you do, it had better be sudden and swift. This beast is extremely dangerous."

"Well, your buddy Carlyle faced it, and he's still around."

"Yes," Giles said with a nod, "in a straitjacket howling his innards out day and night."

*"Okay,* Admiral, way to inspire the troops."

Giles straightened. "Sorry." *Heaven forfend I attempt to inject some gravity into the discussion.*

The sound of the phone slamming down came from the desk. "Xander's not home," Willow said, walking over to join them. "He told his mom he was going to his teacher's house to work on a science project. He didn't tell her where."

*Of course,* Giles thought, remembering his own words. *She lures innocent virgins back to her nest.*

Buffy said, "See if you can get her address off the substitute rolls." She turned to Giles. "And you need to record bat sonar, and fast."

Giles nodded. "Bat sonar, right." Then, realizing he was missing a vital piece of data, he asked, "What?"

"Bats eat them. A mantis hears sonar, its entire nervous system goes kaplooey."

*Kaplooey, slice and dice—these technical terms* will *make my head spin,* Giles thought. "Where am I going to find—?"

"In the vid library," Buffy said, pushing Giles in that direction. "There are no books, but it's still dark and musty, you'll feel right at home. Go!"

Giles went to his office first to get one of the many handheld tape recorders that had been left behind by his predecessor. Behind him, he heard Buffy say, "I guess I'll handle the armory," followed soon after by the sound of his weapons locker opening. Giles found a microtape that he had made some notes on when he first arrived at Sunnydale High and no longer needed, stuck it into the handheld, and then ventured into the video library, where he had to admit he hadn't gone very often. Neither had the students, as it happened—the collection mostly consisted of educational materials that the faculty would use, including, he soon discovered, one on bats.

There was equipment that could make a sophisticated audio recording of something on videotape, but Giles hadn't a clue how to operate it, and there wasn't time in any case. He located the proper tape—noting with sadness that the last person to use the tape, according to the log, was Michael Gregory—and put it in. Once it got round to showing sonar, Giles simply put the handheld to the television speaker and hit play and record.

Ten molar-grinding minutes later, he had recorded what he prayed was enough. He rewound the tape, played enough to hear that it recorded, then noticed that the battery light was flashing. Not wanting the batteries to run dry in the middle of a fight, Giles transferred the tape to another handheld.

He reentered the main part of the library just as the computer printed out a piece of paper for Willow. "Getting the address," she said.

"Great," said Buffy, who was placing her packed duffel on the table. "Giles?"

"Recording bat sonar," he announced while giving Buffy the handheld, "is something soothingly akin to having one's teeth drilled."

"Let's roll," Buffy said.

The three of them headed for the door. As they did, Willow perused the paper she had just liberated from the printer. "According to Ms. French's personnel records, she was born in 1907. She's like ninety years old."

"She is extremely well preserved," Giles said dryly.

It didn't take long to find the French residence at 837 Weatherly Drive. Giles parked in front of the house, and Slayer, Watcher, and student piled out.

"What now?" Giles asked as they approached the door. "We can't just kick the front door down."

"Yeah, that would be wrong," Buffy said just as she prepared to kick the front door down.

Before she could, however, the door opened to reveal a wizened old woman wearing a cardigan sweater and thick, plastic glasses. "Hello, dear," she said. "I thought I heard . . . Are you selling something? Because I'd like to help you out, but you see I'm on a fixed income."

Buffy said slowly, "I'm looking for Ms. French."

"I'm Miss French," the woman said proudly.

"Natalie French," Buffy clarified, "the substitute biology teacher."

"Goodness, that's me," the old woman said with a warm smile. "I taught for over thirty years. I retired in nineteen seventy-two."

Suddenly, everything clicked in Giles's head. Ms. French's record stating that she was born in 1907 made a good deal more sense.

Buffy, having obviously come to the same conclusion, said, "I can't believe this. She used Ms. French's records to get in the school—she could be anywhere."

"No, dear," the old woman said, "I'm right here."

"What do we do now?" Willow asked verging on panic.

"Abject prayer and supplication would spring to mind," Giles muttered. He had to admit to being stumped. He had assumed the She-Mantis's insectoid nature to be responsible for what Buffy would have called "the age thing." The idea of appropriating someone's identity simply hadn't occurred to him.

"I saw her walking past this park with her grocery bags," Buffy said, pointing at the nearby Weatherly Park. "She lives in this neighborhood."

Willow started moving toward one of the other houses. "I'm gonna start banging on doors."

"Wait, no," Buffy said, grabbing her, "we don't have time for that."

"We have to do something!" Willow cried, sounding as pained as Giles had ever heard her. He hadn't realized until that moment just how deep Willow Rosenberg's feelings for Xander were.

"We will," Buffy said, hauling her duffel and heading for the street.

She stopped in front of a sewer cover, dropped the duffel, and pulled out a good length of rope. Then she removed the cover with such ease that Giles had to remind himself how heavy those things actually were.

"I won't be long," she said, and then disappeared into the sewer.

For several tense millennia—though his watch insisted only three minutes passed—Giles and Willow crouched by the sewer opening. At one point, he called her name, but to no response. He wondered what on earth she was doing.

"Come on, Buffy," Willow muttered.

Finally, Giles remembered that their one-handed vampire had taken to living in the sewers. Did she intend to use the so-called "claw guy" as an insect Geiger counter?

He heard the sounds of a struggle in the bushes behind him. As he got up to look, Buffy popped out, along with a large, long-haired vampire whose hands had been tied behind his back. Or, rather, *hand,* singular. "You!" the vampire said, apparently seeing Buffy clearly for the first time.

"Me," Buffy said with a smile. Then she grabbed him from behind and started pushing him down the sidewalk. "Come on, come on, where is she?"

Giles, following behind with Willow, saw that his suspicions were correct. Vampires could obviously sense the She-Mantis's true nature. *Perhaps because her blood is of no use to them.* In any case, Buffy intended to use the vampire to flush her out.

"Which house is it? I know you're afraid of her, I *saw* you. Come on, come on!"

They passed one of those tiresome American split-levels with a white picket fence, and suddenly the vampire tensed.

"What?" Buffy prompted. "What is it? This is the entrance to her house? This is it?"

The vampire said nothing in response, but turned away. Giles then got a glance at the creature's face and—despite what Buffy had said earlier—was shocked to see fear there.

Buffy dragged him closer to the house, saying, "Better than radar." The vampire cringed even more.

The house itself was completely dark, but for a single light coming from a small cellar window.

Giles looked back at the vampire—just as he had finished using his prosthetic to slice through the rope. "Look out!" he cried at the same time that Willow yelled, "Buffy!"

The vampire slashed at Buffy, who sensibly dodged out of the way. Unfortunately, the motion of the dodge caused her to trip and fall on the front lawn. The vampire advanced on Buffy, who crab-walked backward until she ran into the fence.

As Giles debated the wisdom of giving aid, Buffy grabbed a slat of the fence, broke it off in a smooth motion, and used it to stake the vampire.

As the vampire collapsed into dust, Buffy stood up, smiled, and said, "Coming?" Then she made for the house.

*Minimal attention span, perhaps,* the Watcher thought with pride, *but the girl can think on her feet.*

Then he heard the blood-curdling cry for help. . . .

# CHAPTER 6

The big bug opened the door to the cage and motioned for Xander to come out.

*Okay, this is the big moment. This is where you triumph over the forces of darkness and live to fight another day.*

Keeping the purloined cage bar behind his back, he slowly inched feet-first out of the cage. "I'm comin', I'm comin'," he said.

As soon as he was close enough, he slugged the mantis with the bar, then leaped up and ran straight for the stairs.

*I did it! I'm free! I'm gonna be all right—*

A foreleg tripped him, and he came crashing to the stairs with a bone-jarring impact.

*I didn't do it. I'm caught. I'm gonna die.*

The other foreleg grabbed him by the torso and Bug-Lady hefted him with disturbing ease. She carried him to a wall and secured him to it with leather straps. *Just think,* Xander thought bitterly, *if someone told me yesterday that in twenty-four hours Ms. French would be tying me down with leather straps, I'd have been ecstatic.*

"Oh yeah, here it comes," Blayne said.

"What? What's happening?" Xander asked frantically, even though he wasn't one hundred percent sure he really wanted to know.

"How do you like your eggs, bro, over easy or sunny-side up?"

"Eggs? She's gonna lay some—?"

Ms. French's words in bio class several lifetimes ago came back to him: *"The California mantis lays her eggs and then finds a mate to fertilize them."* Hanging from the wall were a bunch of eggs. They were probably the result of her night of passion with the poor schlub in the cage next to Blayne's.

Xander wondered if it was his imagination, but the praying mantis seemed to be smiling. He didn't think bugs could smile.

Then it leaned in closer and said in Natalie French's voice, "Kiss me."

Struggling futilely against his bonds, Xander said, "Can I just say one thing? *Help! Heeeeeeeeelp!*"

As if in response, the small window by the staircase that looked out over the front lawn shattered, and in climbed the most beautiful sight Xander had ever seen in his sixteen years of life:

Buffy.

"Hey, over here!" Blayne cried out. "Hello? In the cage?"

Showing tremendous good sense, Buffy ignored Blayne, instead yelling at the bug, "Let him go!" Buffy had her bag of tricks with her, and pulling out two cans of bug spray, hit the former Ms. French with both barrels.

The smell was terrible, but to Xander it was like roses. The giant bug retreated into a corner.

"Help me!" Blayne continued to wail. "Help me!"

*Lay off, "bro," you're in your cage where it's safe,* Xander thought angrily.

"Get them out of here," Buffy said, and only then did Xander realize that Willow and Giles had followed Buffy through the window. Willow went for the cage and tried to get it open while Giles undid the straps that held Xander.

Buffy then grabbed a handheld tape recorder, of all things, and held it aloft like it was a samurai sword. "Remember Dr. Gregory—you scarfed his head? Yeah, well, he taught me if you do your homework, you learn stuff. Like what happens to your nervous system when you hear *this.*"

She hit the play button.

Rupert Giles's voice said, "—tremely important to file, not simply alphabetically—"

Xander blinked in confusion. *I know what Giles lecturing does to my nervous system, but a mantis's?*

Buffy hit the stop button, crying, "Giles?"

"It's the wrong side," Giles called over.

Then the mantis screeched out of her corner and attacked Buffy, sending the recorder flying across the room and under a refrigerator. Giles went after it. Xander, for his part, went for the cans of bug spray.

Mantis Woman took a swipe at Buffy, which the Slayer leaped over.

The theme from "Mighty Mouse" sounding in his head, Xander then stepped in front of Buffy and hit the mantis with the bug spray.

It only mildly annoyed her this time, and she turned on him. Buffy shoved him rather violently out of the way.

Bug Lady then knocked Buffy down and moved in on her. Buffy got three kicks in, which gave the Slayer a chance to get up.

Then Giles dove in from the back with the recorder in his hand and pushed play.

Xander winced as it played an ear-screeching, high-pitched sound. *What is that?*

The mantis was gyrating around and screeching as if in agony.

As if answering his thought, Buffy said, "Bat sonar makes your whole nervous system go to hell."

She reached into her bag and hefted a giant machete. "You can go there with it."

This time she really did look like a samurai warrior. Xander watched with a combination of revulsion and joy as Buffy took the machete and starting hacking and slashing the giant mantis.

In less than a minute, the floor was covered with mantis chunks.

Standing, brushing himself off, and pocketing the tape recorder, Giles said, "I'd say it's deceased."

"And dissected," Willow added. Xander saw that she had successfully gotten Blayne out of the cage.

# TONIGHT, PART 2

**X**ander Harris had had very few nightmares in his life. Once, toward the end of sophomore year, he'd been given an opportunity to confront one of them: the clown who had provided the "entertainment" for Xander's sixth birthday party.

But one that he doubted would ever leave him was the giant head of a praying mantis leaning in to prepare for a fun-filled evening of mating and decapitation.

He went downstairs for a drink of water. Just thinking about "Ms. French" made his mouth go dry. *Of course,* he thought as he poured from the plastic pitcher his mother kept in the fridge, *some guys might go for something stronger.* But since his primary experience with alcohol involved that selfsame praying mantis, Xander suspected he was going through life as a teetotaler.

Or, at the very least, avoiding martinis like the plague.

As he went back up to his room, he thought about what happened after Ms. French. First Angel revealed himself to be a vampire—but one cursed with a soul, making him a good guy. Sort of. Apparently he ran afoul of a Romany tribe a hundred years back, and this was how the Gypsies punished him. For Xander's part, the idea of cursing someone with goodness struck him as a little wiggy.

So did what happened with Buffy and Angel. She fell head over heels for him, and he fell right back. Even leaving aside Xander's own strong feelings for her, he felt that was just plain wrong. Angel was still a vampire; Buffy was still the Slayer. The only relationship should have been between her stake and his heart. But the lovebirds didn't see it that way. And Xander had to admit that Angel had proven useful against the Master and his henchvamps.

Then came the prophecy. "The Master shall rise and the Slayer shall die."

At first Buffy was understandably resistant to this concept, but eventually she sucked it up and faced the Master. Xander, for his part, saw no reason to let her do it alone. Conscripting Angel to help him, he followed her to the church where the Master was imprisoned—

Too late. When they arrived, the Master was free and Buffy lay face down in a pond, not breathing. Xander refused to accept that she was dead, and gave her mouth-to-mouth and CPR learned at a barely remembered first-aid class at a long-ago summer camp.

But it worked. Buffy coughed and breathed and lived. And then she killed the Master.

At first, things seemed to calm down. Even Cordelia—who had been present for the Master's demise and therefore was now privy to the fact vampires did exist and she was living on the Mouth of Hell—was becoming almost tolerable.

Things, however, never stayed calm on the Hellmouth.

First some vampires tried to resurrect the Master. Then Spike and Drusilla showed up to wreak their little brand of havoc. Then Ampata arrived.

Xander opened his closet door and looked at himself in the mirror on the back of the closet door.

*My clothes are fine. They do make a statement. That statement is, "This is me." And, let's face it, an untucked flannel shirt over an equally untucked T-shirt is me.*

*Certainly Ampata didn't have any problem with it.*

Inside the closet, he noticed the cowboy hat that had been part of the costume he wore for a cultural exchange dance at the Bronze.

Ampata had been his date.

# INCA MUMMY GIRL

## EARLY JUNIOR YEAR

# CHAPTER 1

The good news for Xander was that it was Cultural Exchange Week in Sunnydale. This annual event, instituted by the high school and the City Council several years before, brought foreign students to live in Sunnydale and experience the U.S. of A. firsthand, and also was intended to heighten awareness of other cultures among the American students.

In truth, the event lasted two weeks, but, as Xander pointed out when he and Willow were telling Buffy about it in the library days earlier, "Cultural Exchange Two-Week Period" lacked the proper zing. When Giles said that they could have called it the Cultural Exchange Fortnight, the three teenagers looked at him funny until he went into another room.

Xander loved this event, because it meant that classes were more or less suspended while the great melting pot congratulated itself on how diverse it was for two weeks.

The bad news was that part of the event this year involved a field trip to the Sunnydale Natural History Museum and its Treasures of South America exhibit, a touring show whose arrival at the museum was carefully timed to coincide with Cultural Exchange Week.

Xander used to love field trips, but the last one he went on, to the local zoo, resulted in Xander and four other students being possessed by the spirit of a hyena. The five of them ate a pig whole, and—minus Xander—did likewise for Principal Flutie. As a result, Xander had formed the opinion that field trips were a generally bad idea when one lived on a Hellmouth.

Flutie's somewhat authoritarian replacement, Principal Snyder, didn't go for field trips. It was one of the few things about Snyder that Xander did like. This trip, however, was apparently the exception.

"It's so unfair," Buffy was saying as they approached the large staircase that would bring them into the museum. During the entire bus ride over, she had been complaining because her mother had agreed to house one of the foreign students. Xander had himself been relieved of that option. His parents had expressed a complete lack of interest in, as his father put it, "playing hotel for free for someone who no speaka da language."

"I don't think it's that bad," Willow said.

"It's the *uber*-suck. Mom could have at least warned me."

Xander said, "Well, a lot of the parents are doing it

this year. It's part of this whole cultural exchange megillah: the exhibit, the dance—"

"I have the best costume for the dance," Willow said in an obvious attempt to change the subject.

Buffy, however, didn't take the bait. "A complete stranger in my house for two weeks. I'm gonna be insane. A danger to myself and others within three days, I swear."

"I think the exchange student program is cool," Xander said with all the assurance of someone who didn't have to share his house. When the girls both shot him looks, he added, "I do. It's a beautiful melding of two cultures."

"Have you ever done an exchange program?" Buffy asked.

Xander pretended to consider the question. "My dad tried to sell me to some Armenians once, does that count?"

That, at last, got a smile out of Buffy.

The three of them entered the main hall. Said hall had a dinosaur exhibit. *Why is it,* Xander wondered, *that main halls of natural history museums always have dinosaurs?*

Cordelia was standing by a particularly menacing-looking skeleton, looking over a series of yearbook-style pictures with some of her Cordettes. As Xander, Willow, and Buffy approached, Cordy pointed at one shot and said, "There's mine. Sven. Isn't he lunchable? Mine's definitely the best."

*Of course,* Xander thought. *Her royal heinie has to have the best of everything.*

Buffy walked up to Cordelia and asked, "What are you looking at?"

That, in and of itself, was amazing. A few months ago, Cordy wouldn't have given Buffy the time of day and Buffy would never have asked her for it. But the Slayer had saved Cordelia's life twice, once from a girl who had turned invisible and was terrorizing Cordy and her friends, once from a couple of loony students who wanted to use her head for the Bride of Frankenstein. That, Xander supposed, could thaw even the iciest of relationships. No one would ever accuse them of being friends, but at least they had become civil.

If anyone had asked Xander, he would have said that being civil to Cordelia was a waste of time. But nobody asked him.

"Pictures of our exchange students," was the answer to Buffy's question. Cordelia showed Buffy the photo of Sven, who looked like your basic Norse deity. "Look. One hundred percent Swedish, one hundred percent gorgeous, one hundred percent staying at my house."

They moved on into the South American relics area, which would take them to the special exhibit.

"So," Cordelia asked Buffy, "how's yours? Visually, I mean."

Buffy shrugged. "I don't know. Guy-like."

Xander immediately went to red alert. In all Buffy's moaning about the coming nightmare, the gender of the person never came up. "By 'guy-like,' we are talking big, beefy, guy-like *girl*, right?"

Again, Buffy shrugged. "I was just told, 'guy.'"

Xander was incensed. He couldn't believe that the Slayer, the Chosen One, the kicker of vampire butt, was just meekly accepting this wily, foreign, *male* intruder lying down.

"You didn't look at him first?" Cordelia said, aghast. "He could be dogly." She shook her head. "You live on the edge."

Xander held up his hands. "Hold on a sec. This person who's living with you for two weeks is a man? With man parts? This is a terrible idea!"

"What about the beautiful melding of two cultures?" Willow asked.

"There's no melding, okay?" Xander said forcefully. "He better keep his parts to himself."

Something caught Buffy's attention. "What's he doing?"

Xander followed her gaze to see that Rodney was leaning in too close to one of the exhibits. In fact, it looked like he was scraping it.

"That's Rodney Munson," Xander said as another student walked up to Rodney, who growled, baring his brace-filled teeth. The kid walked away. Rodney was the only person Xander ever knew who looked more intimidating with braces than without. "God's gift to the bell curve," Xander continued. "What he lacks in smarts, he makes up in lack of smarts."

Willow said, in her usual philosophical way, "You just don't like him 'cause of that time he beat you up every day for five years."

"Yeah," Xander said, "I'm irrational that way."

Buffy started to move toward him. "I oughtta stop him before he gets in trouble."

Willow interrupted, stopping Buffy. "I got it. The nonviolent approach is probably better."

As she went off to soothe the savage breast, Buffy said defensively, "I wasn't gonna use violence. I don't always use violence." She turned to Xander and added in a small voice, "Do I?"

Xander put a reassuring hand on her shoulder. "The important thing is, *you* believe that."

He saw Willow approach Rodney, who started another growl, then mellowed when he saw who it was.

"Wha'd you—Oh, Willow, hi."

Shaking his head, Xander chuckled at that sudden change in attitude. While the snobby types like Cordelia tended to snub Will, she managed to ingratiate herself with a number of the school's more Cro-Magnon enrollees by virtue of her tutoring talent.

"That's probably not something you're supposed to be doing," Willow said, indicating Rodney's hand. "You could get in trouble."

Xander now saw that he was holding a penknife and was trying to scrape gold dust off one of the masks. *Ooh, real classy there, Rod.*

Shivering in mock horror, Rodney said, "Oh, no. And they might kick me out of school?"

Willow gamely laughed at that non-witticism, then said, "We still on for our Chem tutorial tomorrow?"

"Yeah. I think I got almost all fourteen natural elements memorized."

"There are a hundred and three," Willow pointed out.

"Oh. So I still got to learn . . . Uh . . ."

"We'll do a touch-up on math, too," Willow said with a smile.

"Thanks."

Before this little exchange between Beauty and the Butt-Head could continue, a voice projected from the entrance to the Treasures of South America exhibit. "Welcome, students. We shall now proceed into the Incan burial chamber. The human sacrifice," the red-jacketed guide added ominously, "is about to begin."

The students all shuffled in. Willow rejoined Xander and Buffy, Rodney went off on his own. They entered a darker room, spotlights illuminating various artifacts. The centerpiece was a giant stone sarcophagus on a raised platform. The trio joined the queue of students lining up to see it.

"Typical museum trick," Xander muttered. "Promise human sacrifice, deliver old pots and pans."

The guide continued his spiel. "Five hundred years ago, the Incan people chose a beautiful teenage girl to become their princess."

Willow whispered, "I hope this story ends with, 'And she lived happily ever after.'"

When they reached the sarcophagus, Xander peered in to see a mummified corpse that looked like it was made of leather. The eye sockets were black, the jaw sunken, and the shriveled arms were holding something that looked like a particularly fancy platter. It reminded Xander of the seder plate Willow had.

"No," Xander whispered back to Willow, "I think it ends with, 'And she became a scary, discolored, shriveled mummy.'"

"The Incan people," the guide continued, "sacrificed their princess to the mountain god Sebancaya. An offering, buried alive for eternity in this dark tomb."

"They could have at least wrapped her in those nice white bandages, like in the movies," Willow said.

The guide went on: "The princess remained there, protected only by a cursed seal, placed there as a warning to any who would wake her."

Part of Xander thought the whole thing was kind of icky. But a much larger part of him was unimpressed. In the last year, he'd seen sights much more bizarre than a long-dead Incan princess ever could be.

Besides, he had other things on his mind.

"So, Buffy, when's exchange-o boy making his appearance?"

"His name is Ampata. I'm meeting him at the bus station tomorrow night."

"Ooh, Sunnydale bus depot. Classy. What a better way to introduce someone to our country than with the stench of urine?"

"Now, if you'll follow me this way, please," the guide said, indicating the way to other Incan treasures.

Rodney couldn't believe how lame the security was in the Natural History Museum. It was like they were asking to get robbed.

The lighting in the South America exhibit was all directed, and the displays were set up on platforms and stuff, so there were tons of dark, shadowy places for Rodney to hide in.

He waited patiently for his fellow students to leave. Then for the museum to close. The only problem with waiting that long was that he was dying for a cigarette. He learned his lesson the last time, though. People noticed the smoke.

It occurred to him that someone might realize that he wasn't on the bus. Then again, most people avoided him. Willow might miss him, but probably nobody else would even notice.

And if they did, who really cared? If that little twerp Snyder called him into his office—again—he'd just say he got lost.

When the doors were all locked, Rodney snuck out of his hiding place. Most of the stuff was behind glass and probably wired with alarms. But the jerks hadn't done anything to protect the mummy.

Or her dish.

The moron in the suit had called it a *cursed seal,* whatever that meant. All Rodney knew was that it looked like something nice. He could probably sell it for some good cash.

"Cool," he said as he reached into the coffin-thing and grabbed for the dish.

Unfortunately, the mummy babe had the dish in a death grip. Rodney pulled on it.

When it finally did come loose, Rodney lost his own hold on it, and it fell to the dais and shattered into a dozen pieces.

"Damn!"

Before Rodney could consider what else he might steal, a wrinkled hand grabbed him by the throat.

It was the mummy. She was choking him.

And her hollow, dead eyes were open.

*But that's impossible,* he thought.

It got harder and harder to breathe.

Then the mummy started to draw him closer.

Rodney didn't have the ability to scream before the rotted lips met his.

# CHAPTER 2

The next day after school, Xander had joined Buffy for her daily workout with Giles in the library. Today, that involved Giles holding one of those big orange pillowlike things that football players crashed into to practice their maiming skills and Buffy attacking it.

Since the moment they arrived, she had been trying to convince Giles to give her the following night off from her usual patrolling to go to the World Culture Dance at the Bronze.

"So," Buffy said after explaining about the dance and how much fun it would be and all the wonderful new cultures she'd be exposed to, "can I go?" She then gave the pillow a good hard kick.

"I think not," Giles said, stumbling with the impact.

Buffy punched the pillow. "How come?"

"Because you are the Chosen One."

Another punch. "Just this once, I'd like to be the Overlooked One." She punctuated this desire with a couple of kicks that made Xander wince.

"I'm afraid," Giles, now wheezing, said, "that is simply not an option. You have responsibilities that other girls do not, and—"

"Oh," Buffy interrupted, "I know this one! 'Slaying entails certain sacrifices, blah blah bliddy-blah, I'm so stuffy, give me a scone.'"

Giles glared at her witheringly. "It's as if you *know* me." But Xander did notice the sheen of sweat on the Watcher's brow. She continued to pummel the pillow with repeated kicks as he went on. "Your secret identity is going to be difficult enough to maintain while this exchange student is living with you."

Xander rolled his eyes. "Not *with* her. In the same house as her. Am I the only one who's objective enough to make that distinction?" He'd been trying to correct this tragic misapprehension all day.

"So then," Buffy said, ignoring Xander in favor of continuing to work on Giles, "going to the dance like a normal person would be the best way to keep that secret." Another kick.

"You're twisting my words," said Giles with a pained grunt.

"No, I'm just using them for good." Another punch. "Giles, come on. Budge. No one likes a nonbudger."

She raised her leg for another kick.

"Fine!" Giles said quickly, backing off from the kick and lowering the pillow. "Go."

"Yay," Buffy said with a smile. "I win."

Dropping the orange pillow to the floor, Giles said, "I think I'll go introduce my shoulder to an ice pack."

As he stumbled off, Xander got up from the desk and said to Buffy, "So, I guess we're dance bound. Cool. I think I can get Mom's car, so I'm Wheel Man."

"I thought you were taking Willow," Buffy said.

"Well, yeah, I'm gonna take Willow, but I'm not gonna *take* Willow. In the sense of 'take me.' See, with you, we're three and everybody's safe. Without you, we're two."

"Ah," Buffy said gravely, "and then we enter Dateville: romance, flowers . . ."

"Lips," Xander added.

"Now, c'mon, in all the years you've known Willow, you've never thought about her lips?"

Xander sighed. This subject always made him uncomfortable. "Buffy, I love Willow, and she's my best friend. Which makes her not the kind of girl who I think about her lips that much." *Ooh, that was coherent,* he thought with an internal sigh. "She's the kind of girl that I'm best friends with."

A voice sounded from the library doors. "Hey, guys."

It was Willow.

Xander panicked. He knew that Willow intellectually understood how Xander felt, but he also knew that emotionally she refused to believe it. It drove Xander nuts, but to pretend he felt otherwise about Willow would just make things worse.

*Maybe she didn't hear us.*

"Willow, hi!" he said a little too loudly. "We were just talking about happy things. Like the three of us going to the dance. See? Happy." Then he finally noticed the sour expression on her face. "Not happy?"

"No. Yes," she quickly added, trying to brighten. Then she dimmed again. "No. Rodney's missing."

Giles walked in on those last two words, holding an icepack to his shoulder. "Trouble with Mr. Munson again?"

"His parents said he never came home last night. The police are still looking for him."

Xander shook his head, relieved that Willow's unhappiness was not because she overheard what he told Buffy. " 'Police are looking for Rodney Munson.' There's a phrase we'll get used to."

Buffy frowned. "You know, I don't remember seeing Rodney on the bus back from the field trip."

"I don't, either," Willow said. "I hope he didn't get into trouble at the museum."

Laughing, Xander said lightly, "Hey, maybe he awakened the mummy."

"Right," Willow said, returning the laugh, "and it rose from its tomb."

Joining in, Buffy added, "And attacked him."

Then they stopped laughing and looked at each other.

Four minds with but a single panic, the students and librarian quickly dashed out of the library, heading for Giles's car, and the museum.

*Field trips on the Hellmouth. Bad idea.* Very *bad idea.*

They arrived within twenty minutes. It would've been sooner, but Giles's car stalled twice. When they got there, the museum was still open, but the South

America exhibit was closed. Luckily, Giles knew one of the curators—"fellow studier of boring, dead things," was Buffy's comment—and she let them in.

"According to Ms. Gilman," Giles said, "the exhibit has been closed since the class left yesterday. It's unlikely that Mr. Munson would have remained unnoticed."

"On the other hand," Willow said, trying to sound hopeful, "maybe Rodney just stepped out for a smoke."

"For twenty-one hours?" Xander asked, his dubiousness muscles on full.

"It's addictive, you know."

Giles said, "We'll deal with that possibility when we've ruled out evil curses."

"Some day," Buffy said wistfully as she approached the sarcophagus, "I'm going to live in a town where evil curses are just generally ruled out without even saying."

"Where was this seal?" Giles asked.

Just as Buffy reached the tomb, she said, "Right here. And it's broken."

Xander walked up to a large piece of the seal that lay on the floor, as well as a couple of shards next to it.

"Does that mean the mummy's loose?" Willow asked.

Both Buffy and Xander peered into the coffin, but the mummy was still lying there, all nice and leathery.

"No," she said. "Comfy as ever."

Giles had, naturally, picked up the large seal fragment. "Look at this series of pictograms . . ."

Before Giles could go off on a no-doubt endless

lecture on the pictograms in question, a man with a machete attacked.

It was a testament to Xander's life these days that a large, scarred man dressed in a loose white shirt and wielding a machete didn't even register as a surprise. The man swung the machete, which Xander ducked under.

The attacker then went for Buffy. Willow hid behind Giles. Buffy also ducked a swipe from the machete, and prepared for another attack.

Then the man looked down into the tomb—and just stopped. Xander took advantage of this opportunity to leap on the guy's back and try to stop him.

The big man then shrugged, removing Xander from his back, and ran off.

"Okay, I just saved us, right?" Xander asked, again utilizing his dubiousness muscles.

"Something did," Buffy said.

"We'll fret about the details later," Giles said. "Let's just get out of here before he comes back."

Xander joined Buffy and Giles in making quickly for the exit. As he did so, he heard Willow's voice from the sarcophagus. "Giles, were the Incas very advanced?"

"Yes. Yes, very," the librarian replied.

"Did they have orthodontists?"

Xander walked back over to the tomb. He looked down to see that, unlike the day before, the mummy had braces.

Rodney Munson's braces.

"Rodney looked like he had been dead for five hundred years. How could that be?"

The ride back from the museum had been fairly silent. It wasn't until they reconvened in the library that Willow asked the question that had been on everyone's mind.

"Maybe," Xander said, "we should ask that crazy man with the big ol' knife."

Buffy said, "I don't think he seemed overly chatty."

"The way he bolted when he saw Rodney," Willow said, "I'd say he was as freaked as we were."

Xander doubted that, but obviously Machete Man hadn't expected Rodney to be in the coffin any more than they all did. He couldn't believe it—Rodney was dead. While Xander had always expected Rodney to die young, he figured it would be in a convenience store holdup or something. *Sometimes I really hate living here.*

"My resources on this subject are extremely limited," said Giles. "I gather that this particular mummy was from the Sebancaya region of eastern Peru. Very remote. If there's an answer, then it's locked—"

"In the seal," Buffy finished.

Giles nodded. "It could take me weeks to translate these pictograms. Well, we'll start tonight with—"

"Ampata!" Buffy cried suddenly, looking stricken.

"I was going to suggest research," Giles said dryly.

Heading for the door, Buffy said, "No, I'm late. I told my mom I'd pick him up."

Xander couldn't believe this. "Buffy, where are your priorities? Tracking down a mummifying killer or making time for some Latin lover whose stock in trade is the breakage of hearts?"

"Ampata is there alone," Buffy said angrily, "and I don't know how good his English is. He's—" suddenly she got a light-bulb-over-the-head look, "from South America. Y'know, maybe he could translate the seal."

Shaking his head, Xander said, "Oh, yeah. Fall for the old let-me-translate-that-ancient-seal-for-you come on. You know how many times I've used that?"

Buffy just glowered at him.

"All right," Xander said, holding his hands up and moving toward the door to join her, "but we're going with you."

Willow blinked. "We are?"

"Fine, whatever, let's *go,*" Buffy said.

Ampata Gutierrez was excited. At last, he had come to America. For years, he had dreamed of this. In sixteen years of life, he had never left Peru. But he had read about other places: Paris, London, New York. Since he was a small boy, he wanted to travel—to see the Eiffel Tower, to explore Buckingham Palace, to climb to the top of the Empire State Building. He wanted to see the entire world.

If he was honest with himself, he would admit that he was, so far, disappointed. Sunnydale, California, had little by way of great sights. Just a lot of small houses that all looked alike. Even Los Angeles, what little of it he saw from the airplane, did not impress him overmuch.

But he refused to let it get him down. He was in America. It was a start. And he was going to make the most of it.

Of course, he could only make the most of it if the girl who was housing him actually turned up. He'd been waiting for half an hour.

"Ampata," a voice whispered.

*Aha,* he thought. *That must be her. But why is she whispering?*

He looked around, but saw no one, aside from the two unshaven men who hadn't moved from the wall they were leaning against since Ampata's arrival.

"Ampata," the voice whispered again. *Does the girl have laryngitis?* Ampata wondered.

This time, though, he had been able to place the voice. He walked around one of the many parked buses to try and locate her.

The buses cast long shadows in the poorly lit depot, so at first Ampata could not make out the figure he saw standing by the bus. He ventured a "Hello?"

Then she stepped into the light.

It was the most hideous creature Ampata had ever seen. It seemed to be vaguely girl-shaped, but horribly wrinkled. It looked like those pictures of lepers Ampata had seen in one of his mother's books.

He started to scream, but the thing grabbed him by the throat, cutting off his breath.

Then that awful face loomed closer and kissed him.

As Ampata Gutierrez felt the life drain from his body, his final thought was, *Now I'll never see Paris.*

# CHAPTER 3

**X**ander never liked the Sunnydale bus depot. This was not odd in any way. Though he'd never taken a poll or anything, he'd certainly never heard a good word about the place. It was dank, badly lit, decorated with furniture and equipment that was state of the art when they put it in in 1953, and had floors that were cleaned once a decade whether they needed it or not.

According to Buffy, Ampata was flying into LAX in Los Angeles, then bussing it here. *Helluva way to introduce someone to this country,* Xander thought. *The world's ugliest airport followed by the world dreariest bus station.*

"Forty minutes late," Buffy muttered. "Welcome to America."

"What if he left already?" Willow asked as they

went outside, not seeing him on any of the steel-and-vinyl benches inside.

Buffy didn't answer Will's question, but instead called out, "Ampata! Ampata Gutierrez!"

They started navigating the parked buses, hoping to see a lost-looking Peruvian. "So," Xander asked, "do we have to speak Spanish when we see him? 'Cause I don't know anything much besides 'Doritos' and 'chihuahua.'"

"Ampata!" Buffy called out again.

"Here," said a small voice.

A small, very female-sounding voice.

Xander looked in the direction of the voice to see, of all things, a girl.

A very beautiful girl. She had lustrous black hair that cascaded down her shoulders like a waterfall. Her almond-colored skin was flawless, and her eyes—

Actually, Xander couldn't see her eyes in this light. But he was quite sure that they were wonderful.

"Hello," she said. "I am Ampata."

"*Ay, caramba,*" he muttered, then added: "I can also say that."

"I'm sorry I'm late," Buffy said apologetically. "I'm Buffy Summers." Buffy reached out to shake her hand.

Ampata blinked for a second, then returned the handshake. "I am very pleased to see you."

"Yeah, I know, I'm *really* sorry for the late thing, but we lost track of time. Oh, uh, these are my friends, Xander Harris and Willow Rosenberg."

Slowly, worried that she might not have very much English, Xander said, "Welcome to our country."

She smiled. She had the most wonderful smile in the world. "Thank you."

"We should get going," Willow said. "After it gets dark, this place stops being a No Big Creepy Weirdos Zone."

After arranging to have Ampata's trunks sent to the Summers house, they piled back into Xander's mother's car, Xander carrying her suitcase to the car himself. The drive was fairly quiet. Ampata seemed enraptured by the houses. Xander wondered as he drove what kind of buildings they had in Peru. *They don't all live in huts still, do they?* He made a mental note to ask Giles the next day.

Buffy gave Ampata the nickel tour of the house upon arrival, ending with the kitchen.

"It is very good," she said when Buffy brought her in. She had said that at every room, in fact.

"Yeah." That was what Buffy had said at every room, also. "You got your stove, your fridge—it's fully functional, we're very into it."

"Would you like a drink?" Xander asked, once again being sure to enunciate.

"Let's see," Buffy said, peering into the fridge, "we've got milk, and . . . older milk. Juice?"

"Please," Ampata said, sitting at the kitchen counter. Xander sat on the stool next to her.

"So," Willow said, "Ampata. You're a girl."

She gave that amazing smile again as she replied, "Yes, for many years now."

"And not a boy," Willow added. "'Cause we thought a boy was coming, and there you are in a girl way."

101

Xander wondered how this was relevant. "Just one of those crazy mix-ups, Will."

Buffy handed Ampata a glass of apple juice and asked, "So, have you been to America before?"

"I have—toured."

Again enunciating to make sure she understood, Xander asked, "Where did you go?"

"I was taken to Atlanta, Boston, New York . . ."

Willow brightened. "New York? That's exciting. What was that like?"

Xander smiled to himself. Will had always wanted to visit New York.

"I did not see so much," Ampata said, and Willow noticeably deflated.

"Your English is very *bueno*," Xander said.

Again Ampata smiled. "I listen much."

"Well, that works out well, 'cause I talk much."

Both Xander and Ampata laughed at that.

Buffy sat in her bedroom, having moved a cot in for Ampata. It had practically taken an act of God to get Xander to finally leave, but Willow eventually managed to drag him out, with a significant push from Mom, who made it clear that she was exhausted and wanted to sleep.

Mom, however, wasn't too exhausted to make up the extra bed, and also to suggest that Ampata share Buffy's room, since she was a girl rather than the expected boy who was going to sleep in the living room.

Buffy wasn't sure how she felt about that. Her Slaying was going to be screwed enough just having Ampata around generally. Putting her in the same room was going to cut it off all together. As well as Angel's visits to her window late at night . . .

*Oh well. No one said life was fair. If it was, I wouldn't worry about how a houseguest is interfering with my going out and staking vampires in the first place.*

"Sorry about the teeniness of the room," Buffy said. The second bed reduced the floor space to almost nothing.

"My old one was much smaller," Ampata said.

"What's it like, back home?"

"Cramped. And very dead."

Buffy smiled. "Well, you'll feel right at home in Sunnydale."

"Oh, no, but you have so much here."

This surprised Buffy. Ampata had been fairly reserved, and given seriously short answers to everything. Buffy assumed at first that it was a language thing, though her English was just fine.

But suddenly she was very emphatic about how much they had in Sunnydale.

*The only thing we have "so much" of is ickiness.*

Ampata had walked over to the desk where a picture of Buffy, Willow, and Xander that Willow's mother had taken last year sat in a wooden frame.

Buffy asked, "How about friends?"

"They are—" Ampata hesitated.

*Struggling for the right words in English, or is it something else?* Buffy wondered, then chastised herself. *You're too suspicious. Not everything is a crazed demon out to wipe out the human race. It's just a kid from another country.*

"It's just me," Ampata finally said.

*Just a* lonely *kid from another country.* Buffy knew the emotion behind Ampata's words. She remembered the other students at Hemery High after the gymnasium burned down and she was expelled. The same kids who had been her closest friends wouldn't speak to her, some crossing the street to avoid her.

"I've been there," Buffy said with feeling. "But hey, you'll meet lots of people tomorrow."

"Thank you," Ampata said, climbing into the spare bed. "You must teach me everything about your life. I want to fit in, Buffy. Just like you. A normal life."

*Girl, you have no idea what you're asking.* But aloud, she just said, "One normal life, coming up."

# CHAPTER 4

Oz wasn't exactly upset. This was because Oz didn't get upset. Getting upset usually required more energy than Oz was willing to expend. But if he had been willing to expend that energy, he would've done so on Devon right now.

Here they were, loading their band equipment into Oz's van to take to the Bronze for tonight's World Culture Dance, and their lead singer was busy talking to his girlfriend.

Of course, had Oz actually been upset, it probably would've been more due to the fact that Oz didn't have a girlfriend of his own to be distracted by. It's not like Devon ever carried the heavy stuff anyhow. And it was hard to ignore Cordelia Chase when she wanted to talk to you. Kinda like trying to ignore a tornado, if a tornado wore mascara and pumps.

Still, playing the World Culture Dance at the Bronze was a major coup for Dingoes Ate My Baby, and Oz thought Devon should carry his own weight. Or, at least, *some* of the equipment.

"Devon," Cordelia was saying, "I told you I'd be at the dance tonight, but I'm not one of your little groupies. I won't be all doe-eyed, looking up at you, standing at the edge of the stage."

"Got it," Devon said.

"So, I'll see you afterward?"

"Sure. Where do you want to meet?"

"I'll be standing at the edge of the stage."

Oz considered laughing, then decided that it would be cruel.

Devon, who naturally missed the irony entirely, pointed at a blond-haired giant who stood by the staircase like a Swedish Lurch. "With that guy?"

Cordelia turned to the Thor wannabe. "Sven, momento. Needa." Then she turned back to Devon. "This whole student exchange thing has been a horrible nightmare. They don't even speak American!" She kissed Devon on the cheek. "So, I'll see you later. 'Bye!" Then she turned once again to Nordic Man and spoke as if to a dog. "Sven. Come."

Sven followed Cordelia off to wherever. Devon walked over to Oz.

"Oz, man, what do you think?"

"Of what?"

"Cordelia, man."

Oz considered several responses, rejected most of them as being nonconducive to keeping a perfectly good lead singer, and opted for: "She's a wonderland tour."

"You gotta admit, the girl is hot."

"Yeah, a hot girl," Oz deadpanned.

"Let me guess, not your type?" Devon smiled. "What does a girl have to do to impress you?"

Since a straight answer would go right over Devon's head, Oz replied, "Well, it involves a feather boa and the theme from *A Summer Place*. I can't discuss it here."

Devon shook his head. "You're too picky, man. You know how many girls you could have? You're lead guitar, Oz, that's *currency*."

"I'm not picky. You're just impressed by any pretty girl that can walk and talk."

Devon innocently said, "She doesn't have to talk."

Oz gave up.

Willow had met up with Xander in the morning, as she often did, and they started talking about that evening's dance.

On several occasions, Willow considered bringing up the subject of the two of them going together, just to see his reaction. But she didn't. Xander hadn't realized that she'd heard every word he'd said to Buffy yesterday, and Willow had decided, reluctantly, that it was probably better that way.

"I worked really hard on my costume," she said instead. "It's pretty cool."

"Okay, but what about me? I gotta think."

*Typical,* Willow thought. Xander had left his costume until the last minute. *If they ever start a Procrastinator's Club on campus, Xander would be the first in line to not get around to joining it.*

"It's a celebration of cultures," she said. "There are lots of dress-up alternatives."

"And a corresponding equal number of mocking alternatives, all aimed at me."

Willow considered. She got a mental image of Xander in a ruffled shirt, one of those hats with feathers, and lederhosen. She liked the image a lot, particularly his legs in the lederhosen. "Bavarians are cool."

"Okay, no shirts with ruffles," Xander said emphatically, "no hats with feathers, and *definitely* no lederhosen. They make my calves look fat."

Willow sighed. "Why are you suddenly so worried about looking like an idiot?" She cast her mind back over what she just said. "That came out wrong."

But Xander wasn't even listening. Instead, he was staring. Willow followed his gaze to see what he was staring at, even though she already knew in her gut what it was.

As expected, Ampata and Buffy had just come into sight. Normally, Willow would expect Xander to be mooning after Buffy, but now he only seemed to have eyes for Ampata. It had almost been embarrassing watching him fawn all over her last night.

Again, Willow sighed.

"Your first day of school," Buffy said with a smile. "Nervous?"

Ampata looked overwhelmed. "It is just more people than I have seen in a long time."

"Ah, don't worry. You'll have no problems making friends. As a matter of fact, I know someone who's dying to meet you."

She caught sight of Xander and Willow, and they paused to say hi to each other. Xander barely noticed Buffy, focusing instead on Ampata. The Slayer didn't know whether to be relieved or insulted.

Xander also barely noticed Willow, who stood to the side with her sad face on.

Buffy asked Will a question about the Chem homework to distract her, and it seemed to work. As Xander and Ampata talked about how she slept the previous night, Buffy pretended to be fascinated with the details of carbon atoms.

They went to homeroom, which was crowded with half a dozen foreign extras, then onward and downward to their first couple of classes. Ampata took everything in with an almost-zealous fascination. The teachers all seemed to take a shine to her, as well.

Buffy, Willow, and Xander all had the same free period, which traditionally meant going to the library to check in with Giles. Buffy explained to Ampata that they were on their way to the man who was dying to meet her. Ampata got another one of her strange looks at that.

When they arrived, the Watcher was, conveniently, standing over the largest unbroken piece of the seal. "Ampata," Buffy said, "this is our school librarian, Mr. Giles."

"Hello," Ampata said.

"How do you do?" Giles said, shaking her hand. Then he held out the seal. "I was wondering if you could translate this?"

Buffy blinked. "That was in no way awkward," she said sarcastically.

Ampata, however, did take a look at the seal, and

got another weird look on her face. But it wasn't the embarrassment or confusion Buffy would have expected from Giles's severe lack of tact. "Something wrong?" Buffy asked.

Shaking her head, Ampata said, "No, it is—why are you asking me?"

"Well, it's an artifact," Giles said, "from your region. It's from the tomb of an Incan mummy, actually. We're trying to translate it as a project for our . . ." The librarian trailed off.

"Archaeology club," Willow said quickly.

"Very good," Giles muttered. Obviously he hadn't thought his spiel through.

"It is broken," Ampata said. "Where are the other pieces?"

"This is the only one we found," Buffy said. Not entirely true, but the other fragments were too small to be especially useful.

"It is very old. Valuable." She thought for a moment, then: "You should hide it."

"Is there anything you recognize here?" Giles asked, pointing at one of the figures. "This chappie with the knife?"

"Well, I do not know exactly, but I think this represents—I believe the word is, bodyguard?"

Giles nodded. "Bodyguard. Interesting."

"Legend has it," Ampata continued, "that he guards the mummy against those who would disturb her."

"By slicing them up?" Buffy asked.

"I would not know that."

Giles set the fragment down on the desk. "Yes, well,

that's a very good starting point for our . . . club." He looked at Buffy.

It took Buffy a minute to figure out the look, but then she quickly said, "Oh! And, as club president, I have lots to do—lots of stuff. Dull stuff." She looked at Willow. "Willow, maybe you could—"

Xander interjected, "Stay with Ampata for the day?" He offered her his arm. "I'd love to."

Ampata smiled. "Yes, that will be fun."

He led her out the door.

"Right," Giles said after an awkward silence. "I'll continue with the translation. Buffy, you research this bodyguard thing. And, Willow? Willow?"

Buffy saw that Willow was still staring at the door through which Xander and Ampata had left. "Boy, they really like each other," she said in a tone that made Buffy's heart break.

Xander had never experienced anything quite like this day before. True, he had lusted after various women, from the crush he had on his first-grade teacher all the way through to Buffy. Not to mention Ms. French.

But today with Ampata was the first time he'd had the opportunity to engage in what his grandfather referred to as the lost art of courting. For the first time in his life, Xander had been given the opportunity to flirt for more than seven and a half seconds without being laughed at. Not only was Ampata enjoying it, she even seemed to be flirting back. The novelty of this experience made Xander's head spin.

Ampata went with him to his remaining classes.

She gagged her way through the cafeteria food at lunchtime—though she insisted it wasn't that bad, to Xander's utter shock. After school ended, he continued the tour of the grounds, ending up at the bleachers. They had the place to themselves, aside from a Go Razorbacks! banner, since the football team had an away game this afternoon.

As they took seats near the top of the bleachers, Xander reached into his backpack. He had been lecturing Ampata about American food, wanting her to understand that the swill from the cafeteria was not the usual thing. "And this," he said with a certain amount of drama, "is called a snack food." He held up a Twinkie.

"Snack food," Ampata repeated, sounding a bit dubious.

"Yeah, it's a delicious, spongy, golden cake, stuffed with a delightful creamy white substance of goodness. And here's how you eat it."

Then, in a maneuver that had never failed in over ten years to make Willow wince, Xander shoved the entire Twinkie into his mouth.

Ampata did not wince. She did laugh. Xander liked her laugh.

"Oh, but now I cannot try it."

Holding up his left finger, Xander dipped into his backpack with his right hand. His words barely comprehensible with a mouth full of creamy white substances of goodness, he said, "That's why you bring two."

He whipped out another Twinkie and handed it to her.

Ampata held it with appropriate reverence. "Here goes."

She stuffed it into her mouth whole. Unfortunately, then she started laughing, thus almost spitting the entire thing out.

"Good, huh?" Xander said, also laughing. "And the exciting part is, they have no ingredients that a human can pronounce. So it doesn't leave you with that heavy, food feeling in your stomach."

Smiling after swallowing her Twinkie, Ampata said, "You are strange."

"Girls always tell me that right before they run away," Xander said, truthfully.

"I like it."

*No girl has ever said that,* Xander thought with glee. "I like you like it." He thought back over his words, then added, "Please don't learn from my English."

Again, she laughed. Again, he returned the laugh.

*I could get used to this.*

And again, they were attacked by the large man with the poofy shirt and the big knife.

"You stole the seal!" the man cried. "Where is it?"

Xander fell off the bleacher bench and onto his back on the next row down.

Their attacker leaped down after him and was about to filet Xander with the machete. Running on autopilot, Xander instinctively reached up to grab the man's forearm in order to block his attack.

To Xander's amazement, this actually worked. But the man was impossibly strong, and Xander was going to lose the grip in a minute unless he did something.

Then Ampata screamed.

The bodyguard—if that's what he truly was—looked over at Ampata for the first time, and then his eyes grew wide. "It *is* you!" he said, whatever that meant.

Taking advantage of this distraction, Xander kicked the guy in the stomach. As he went rolling down the remaining bleachers, Xander clambered to an upright position, grabbed his backpack with one hand and Ampata's arm with the other. "Come on," he said as he led her back to the school.

# CHAPTER 5

Buffy sat staring at some pictures in one of Giles's books. She had a large magnifying glass over it so she could make out the details, in the hopes of finding something similar to what was on the seal fragment.

She'd spent most of her free period finding absolutely nothing, and she and Willow had returned at lunch to find more absolutely nothing. The third round of nothing was now coming after school. Times like this, she really respected Giles. He did this sort of stuff all the time, and even though he obviously enjoyed it more than she did, it still had to be frustrating. Digging around through endless texts in the fond hope of finding something useful, and not actually finding anything, couldn't have been exactly what you'd call uplifting.

Buffy decided she liked her end of Slaying better.

Find the target, nail the target. Simple, straightforward.

Then she noticed something. "Hah!" she cried. Then she looked more closely at it. "Or, possible hah." She turned the book around to face Willow, who sat opposite her. "Do you think this matches?"

Willow did not reply. She was, in fact, staring off into space while twirling a stuffed animal. Again. She'd been like this ever since Xander went off with Ampata in the morning. "Hey," Buffy prompted.

Suddenly, Willow came out of it. "Oh! Yes, I'm caring about mummies."

Again, Buffy's heart broke. "Ampata's only staying two weeks."

"Yeah," Willow said bitterly. "And then Xander can find someone else who's not me to obsess about. At least with you I knew he didn't have a shot."

Buffy bit her lip. It had been difficult for her to turn down Xander's invitation to the prom, and all his other advances, but she just didn't feel that way about him. *Listen to me,* she thought, *I'm sounding just like Xander did yesterday. Great little love triangle we've got going here, huh?*

As Giles entered and peered at Buffy's book, Willow put on her brave face and said, "Well, you know, I have a choice. I can spend my life waiting for Xander to go out with every other girl in the world until he notices me, or I can just get on with my life."

Buffy smiled. She'd been waiting months to hear these words from Willow. "Good for you."

The brave face fell. "Well, I didn't choose yet."

Sighing, Buffy was about to launch into a pep talk,

when Giles said, "Good Lord." Then he looked at Buffy. "Good work."

Buffy blinked in pleased surprise. "My work?"

"Yes. This is most illuminating." He pointed at the picture in the book, which was, as Buffy had thought, a more detailed rendering of something on the seal. "It seems that Rodney's killer might be the mummy."

Willow leaned forward, looking at the book. "Where does it say that?"

Giles repositioned the book so that Willow could get a better view. "Here. It implies that the mummy is capable of feeding on the life force of a person. Effectively freeze drying them, you might say. Extraordinary."

Buffy leaned back in her chair. "So now we just have to stop the mummy. Which leaves the question, how do we a, find and b, stop the mummy?"

Straightening up, Giles said, "Well, the answer to that is somewhere still in here. Or in the rest of the seal."

Before the conversation could continue, Xander and Ampata came in, all out of breath. "Machete Boy's back," Xander said before anybody could say anything, "and there's gonna be trouble."

Xander seemed to be okay, but Ampata looked devastated. Xander explained what happened at the bleachers. As he did so, Giles put on some tea. *What is it about Brits that their solution to everything is tea?* Buffy wondered, not for the first time.

When the tea was ready, Giles handed Ampata a mug. "Here you are."

"Why is this guy so into us?" Willow asked. "What's he want?"

Xander shrugged. "He said, 'You stole the seal.'"

"Apparently," Giles said, now holding the seal fragment, "this is more popular than we realized. I just don't know what we should do with it."

For the first time since Xander led her in, Ampata spoke. "Destroy it. If you do not, someone could die."

"I'm afraid someone already has," Giles muttered.

Alarm bells went off in Buffy's head but Ampata only said, "You mean the man with the knife killed someone?"

"No," Buffy said. "Well, not exactly."

"You are not telling me everything," Ampata said, and once again Buffy found herself thinking that Ampata didn't know the half of what she said.

Before anybody else could speak, Xander took Ampata's hands in his and said, "You're right, Ampata. And it's time we do. We're not in the Archaeology Club. We're in—"

More alarm bells went off in Buffy's head, and Giles pointedly cleared his throat. She couldn't believe that Xander would be so idiotic as to tell everything to Ampata.

"We're in the Crime Club," Xander said, barely missing a beat, and Buffy allowed herself to exhale. "Which is kinda like the Chess Club, only with crime, and no chess."

"Please understand me," Ampata said, getting up. "That seal nearly got us killed. It must be destroyed!"

And with that, she turned and ran out of the library.

"Ampata!" Xander called, and ran after her.

Willow then followed Xander out.

*And the love triangle just rolls merrily along,* Buffy

thought, then considered that triangles didn't, generally, roll.

Willow ran out of the library just as Xander found Ampata standing against the wall in the now-deserted hallway. Luckily, very few students stayed after school, except for sporting events, and with the football team away, that just left detention-goers, a few extracurricular activities, and Slayerettes.

"Ampata, listen to me," Xander was saying. "Nobody's going to hurt you. I won't let them."

"Your investigation is dangerous," she said, and Willow noticed that she was crying. "I do not want that. Just normal life."

She turned and went over to the water fountain. Willow came up behind Xander and asked, "Is she okay?"

"Wigged," Xander said. "I'm trying to convince her that our lives aren't just danger and peril around here."

Willow resisted the obvious reply and instead said the words that she knew she had to say even though she would rather rip her own lungs out than actually say them. "You should take her to the dance."

Xander shot her a look. "That's a good idea. We'll all go."

"No, I mean just you."

"But you were psyched," Xander said, sounding confused. "And your costume—"

"I'll see you there."

A moment, then Xander broke into a huge smile. "You know what, Willow? You're my *best* friend."

With that, he went over to Ampata. Willow waited

until she was sure he was out of earshot, then said quietly, "I know."

After Ampata, Xander, and Willow each departed the library in succession, Giles turned his attention back to the seal. He was grateful, actually, that he had been left alone with Buffy. She at least seemed to be one step removed from the bizarre mating ritual that was going on among the other three. Raging teenage hormones tended to give him a headache. He had thought that his relationship with computer teacher Jenny Calendar—which was proceeding very nicely—would make him more tolerant of the odd love triangles that seemed to dog Buffy and her friends, but if anything it made him less so.

"I don't get it," Buffy said, and Giles turned his attention back to the seal as she spoke. "Why would the bodyguard have a Jones for a broken piece of rock?"

"Well, um, perhaps he needs to put it together with the other pieces."

*"If* he has them," Buffy said. "I mean, we didn't find them all."

Giles considered the point. He also considered their hasty retreat from the Treasures of South America exhibit. "If he didn't, then they'd still be at the museum."

"So maybe we should go there and find them. Odds are, he'll show up too, right?"

Nodding, Giles said, "And hopefully, we'll be ready." Buffy hadn't really had a chance to properly face this bodyguard chap. Giles suspected he had no

Xander

"I think the whole sucking-the-life-out-of-people thing would have been a strain on the relationship."
—Xander

"I remember begging you to undress me . . .
and then a sudden need for cheese."
—Buffy

references that littered Xander's conversations, the princess caught sight of her destination. Smiling coyly, she said, "I will return to you."

"Where are you going?"

"Where you cannot follow," she said ominously.

With that, she opened the door to the girls' restroom.

"I'll wait outside," Xander said.

She went in, eventually winding up at the mirror to comb her hair. She gazed upon her reflection and smiled. She looked happy. She looked content. *Good. One should look how one feels.*

But she also was starting to look pale. *No,* she thought. The two lives she took should have been enough to last her. She looked at her hands to see that the skin was becoming less smooth.

*No! It's not fair!* She did not want to take any more lives, but she didn't want to go back to that hellish existence in the sarcophagus. She wanted to live.

She looked up at her reflection in the mirror again—to see the Guardian standing behind her.

The princess whirled around to face him and spoke in a very old language. "I beg you, do not kill me."

The Guardian replied in the same tongue. "You are already dead. For five hundred years."

"But it was not fair," she pleaded. "I was innocent."

"The people you kill now so that you may live, *they* are innocent."

The princess winced. "Please. I am in love."

She surprised herself with her words, but as soon as she spoke them, she knew they were true. She loved Alexander Harris. For all her life, she had been treated with the odd kind of reverence reserved for religious icons. She wasn't a human being, she was the sacrifice. Xander was the first one to treat her like an actual person, and she would always love him for that.

The Guardian came closer. "You are the Chosen One. You must die. You have no choice."

The princess looked down and saw that her hands grew more wrinkled. She would need to feed on someone, and soon.

She looked up. *Why not solve two problems at once?*

The Guardian raised his right arm. In his hand he held a dagger. But as he thrust that arm downward, the princess caught it with her right hand, redirected it, and twisted the Guardian's arm behind his back. With her left hand, she cupped the surprised Guardian's face.

"I do," she said, determined.

Then she kissed him. She felt the life flow from him into her.

Within seconds, it was over. *And the Guardian is a mystical creature. His life should suffice for a long time.* At least, she hoped so.

After moving the now-mummified corpse into one of the stalls, she went back outside to see Xander sitting nervously on one of the benches. Upon seeing her, he stood up.

"I have thought," she said. "The dance. I will go with you. Gladly."

Xander broke into a huge smile. He took her hand in his, and they walked on down the hallway.

*Now, at last, I can be happy.*

# CHAPTER 6

Ampata came into the bedroom from the bathroom and said, "Buffy, I cannot find lipstick."

Buffy looked up. Ampata was in costume and she almost looked like the perfect Incan princess. The only thing missing was, in fact, lipstick. "Oh, you can borrow one of mine," she said. "There should be one on the desk."

Ampata looked at the trunks that took up what little floorspace had remained in the room. "What is that?"

"The station sent the rest of your stuff."

"Oh, of course. I forgot all about it. I will unpack it later."

"No worries. I can do it."

Ampata frowned and looked over Buffy, who was

wearing a T-shirt and overalls. "But you must get ready for the dance."

*And thank you for the reminder,* Buffy thought bitterly, but bit back saying it out loud. It wasn't Ampata's fault that her Watcher was a mean, tweedy old guy with no understanding of the finer things in life. Like dances. And fun.

"I'm not going."

"Why not?" Ampata sounded stunned.

"I have work to do. Crime Club work. It's really nothing for you to worry about."

She smiled. "I am not worried. Thanks to Xander."

"He seems very happy around you."

"I am happy, too," she said. "He has a way of making the milk come out of my nose."

Buffy grinned. "And that's good?"

"From making me laugh," Ampata explained as she walked over to Buffy's desk. She rummaged around the desk and found some cherry red lipstick. "This one?"

"Oooh, no, that clashes. There should be a gold one in there somewhere."

"Thank you," Ampata said with a warm smile. "You are always thinking of others before yourself. You remind me of someone from very long ago. The Inca princess."

Buffy liked the sound of that. "Cool. A princess." She got up and walked over to Ampata's luggage.

"They told her that she was the only one, that only she could defend her people from the netherworld."

As Ampata spoke, Buffy took a quick look in the suitcase—and was surprised to find boys' briefs in

Ampata's luggage. *What?* Then she noticed that Ampata had opened the drawer where Buffy kept her stakes and crucifixes. *Knew I should've moved that stuff to the closet.*

"Out of all the girls in her generation, she was the only one—"

"Chosen," Buffy finished while closing the drawer, suddenly not liking the sound of that so much. *How much does she know?*

"You know the story?" Ampata asked, surprised.

Buffy was grateful for that surprise, though between that and the male underwear, she was starting to seriously wonder about this girl. Aloud she said simply, "It's fairly familiar." She saw the lipstick hiding under some necklaces, including the cross necklace Angel had given her the first time they met, and handed it to Ampata.

"She was sixteen, like us," Ampata said as she took the tube from Buffy. "She was offered as a sacrifice and went to her death. Who knows what she had to give up to fulfill her duty to others? What chance at love?"

Buffy thought about Angel. True, theirs was an odd relationship, a Slayer loving a vampire with a soul. But they had a chance. It was possible. Besides, she'd already beaten one prophecy that said she would die. Clinging to that, she said, "Who knows?"

She walked over to the larger trunk and said, "I'll just unpack the rest of your stuff for you."

Just as she started to open the trunk, however, the doorbell rang. Letting the lid fall, she said, "That's Xander and Willow. I'll get it."

Buffy dashed downstairs and opened the door to a cowboy. It was Xander, dressed like Clint Eastwood in *A Fistful of Dollars*. Buffy wondered if he'd gone so far as to wear the metal plate under his poncho in order to stop bullets.

Speaking in a monotone through teeth clenched over an unlit cheroot, Xander said, "I have come for the dance."

"And what culture are you?" Buffy asked with a grin.

"I am from the country of Leone." Then Xander removed the cheroot and returned to his normal voice. "It's in Italy, pretending to be Montana." He looked up and down at Buffy. "And what are you from, the country of white trash?"

Sighing, Buffy said, "New lineup. You and Willow are taking Ampata. Giles and I are hunting mummies." She peered past Xander, but there was no Willow to be found. "Where's you and Willow?"

"She's not coming with us."

"Oh," Buffy said, nodding. "On a date. Romance, lips."

Xander looked like he was about to reply, but something caught his eye on the staircase. Buffy followed his gaze to see Ampata walking down the stairs. The lipstick definitely was the final missing piece to make her look gorgeous.

"Hello, Xander," Ampata said.

"Ah, yiyuh."

"I can translate American Salivating Boy Talk," Buffy said as Ampata came to the foot of the staircase. "He said you're beautiful."

"Hajya," Xander said to Buffy.

"You're welcome," Buffy replied.

Joyce Summers came in then. "Ampata, don't you look wonderful? I wish you could talk my daughter into going with you."

"I tried," Ampata said. "But she is very stubborn."

Chuckling, Mom said, "I'm glad someone else sees that."

"Well, good night, then," Ampata said, moving to the doorway.

Xander put his hand on Buffy's shoulder and whispered, "Be careful."

"I will," she replied in similarly hushed tones. *Hopefully, Mom didn't hear, or at least figured it's weird teenage code.* "Hey," she added as Xander turned to leave. When he stopped and turned back, she said, "You look good."

He smiled, then went out with Ampata.

Mom walked up behind Buffy, watching them go off together to Xander's mother's car. "Look at that," Mom said. "Two days in America, and Ampata already seems like she belongs here. She's really fitting in."

"Yeah," Buffy said wistfully. "How about that?"

Cordelia went into the Bronze and saw that no one else had gone for the Hawaiian look. *Good,* she thought. She had no worries that she would be anything less than the most gorgeous person there.

Especially given her outfit: a blue bikini top with a stylized white flower pattern, a matching sarong, a pink-and-white *lei,* and a pink hibiscus flower in her hair. Still within the bounds of decency, but showing more than enough to put her fabulous body on display.

Of course, Mother had to be annoying and point out that Hawaii wasn't really another culture, since it was technically part of the United States. Cordelia thought that was silly. *After all,* she thought, *in Hawaii they look different, talk funny, and have weird names.* As far as she was concerned, that made it another culture. If it came to that, Cordelia felt the same way about Texas.

As she entered, she caught sight of Willow and had to keep herself from laughing. Then, realizing there was no reason not to, she went ahead and laughed. Willow had dressed in an eskimo outfit, complete with furry hood and spear. With all the people in the Bronze, it had to be like a million degrees in the outfit.

Cordelia had always thought that the smarter you were, the more clueless you were. How else to explain why Willow, who was one of the school brainiacs, would wear so dorky and concealing an outfit?

Deciding that laughter wasn't nearly enough, Cordelia said as she passed by, "Ooh, near *faux pas.* I almost wore the same thing."

Willow just stood there, holding her spear. It's possible she made a face, but it was hard to tell under all that fur.

*Sometimes,* Cordelia thought, *it's just too easy.*

She found Gwen sitting by the staircase, dressed like something Japan-ish. On the stage, Devon's band was playing a song that was dance-able, but not obnoxiously loud or fast.

Gwen asked, "Hey, where's Sven?"

Cordelia groaned. She'd managed to go a whole minute without thinking about her big, dumb, Swedish appendage. "I keep trying to ditch him, but he's like one of those dogs you leave at the Grand Canyon on vacation. It follows you back across four states."

As if on cue, Sven, dressed like a Viking warrior, walked up to her. "See? My own speechless, human boomerang."

"He's kind of cute," Gwen said. "Maybe it's nice, skipping all that small talk."

Gwen had a point, Cordelia had to admit, remembering some lame conversations with Devon. Still . . . "Small talk? How about simple instructions?" She gestured at Sven. "Get punch-y? You? Fruit drinky?"

Sven didn't move.

Gwen got up and grabbed Sven's arm. "He can follow me."

Willow stood sweltering in her furry outfit. It had seemed like such a good idea at the time. She had researched a variety of *esquimaux* tribes, put together an authentic Inuit parka made from something that looked as much like caribou pelt as she could manage using materials available in a suburban mall, and even modeled her spear after an old engraving she'd found in one of Giles's books.

It never occurred to her that wearing a fur-lined parka made of imitation caribou pelt in the middle of a crowded Bronze would be the textbook definition of *uncomfortable.*

And she was here by herself. True, it was her idea to come by herself so that Xander would be happy, but that didn't exactly cheer her up.

Neither had Cordelia's cheap shot. She tried not to let Cordelia get to her. All Cordelia had going for her was the fact that she was incredibly popular and drop-dead gorgeous, whereas Willow had—

Well, she was sure she had something Cordelia didn't. If it took till the day she died, she was sure she'd find it.

Then Ampata and Xander walked in.

Willow, unable to see past the *faux* fur lining of her hood, had to pivot her torso in order to see what everyone else was looking at. What they looked at was Ampata, who looked simply gorgeous in her Inca princess outfit. Not only that, but it looked authentic, as Willow had learned from spending a day perusing various texts on the ancient Incas.

Looking down at her own, bulky outfit, she sighed and muttered, "I guess I should have worn something sexy."

Xander caught sight of Willow and led Ampata over to her. He was dressed as a cowboy, and he looked wonderful, too. But then, to Willow, he always did.

"Wow," Willow said, "you guys look great."

"I love your costume," Ampata said. "It's very authentic."

*Well, at least she noticed,* Willow thought, but it was small comfort. "Thanks," she muttered.

"Yeah," Xander agreed, "you look, uh—snug."

"That's what I was going for," Willow said, hoping she sounded convincing. "Where's Buffy?"

"Crime Club stuff," Xander said quickly. "Giles had something that had to be done right away. You know how these faculty advisers get."

Willow tried to nod, found she couldn't in the hood, and so said, "Oh."

The song ended, which Willow only noticed because people applauded. She honestly hadn't really noticed the band. After the applause died down, they started a slow dance number.

Xander looked at Ampata. "Do you, uh—would you like to, uh, you know . . ."

"I'd love to dance," Ampata said, saving Xander some embarrassment.

Smiling, Xander led her to the dance floor.

Again, Willow sighed.

Oz scanned the crowd. This particular song was pretty straightforward. It was a ballad with no changes and a bunch of open chords that Oz could pretty much do in his sleep. Oz didn't much care for ballads, but at a dance like this, you had to cater to the crowd.

Oz scoped out the people. He'd never seen so many costumes before when it wasn't Halloween. He had to admit, it looked pretty cool.

Two things grabbed his attention. The first was hard to miss, 'cause everyone else was looking at them, too: a couple who were dancing in the middle of the floor. The woman was dressed up as some kind of South American goddess, and the guy was a cowboy. Most people were just dancing normally, but these two were completely locked into each other. It was like something out of *West Side Story*.

The second thing was just beyond them. It was a girl wearing an eskimo suit. It was the cutest thing he'd ever seen in his life.

Oz had seen the couple on the floor and moved on. But this girl completely—and uncharacteristically—had him riveted.

They had gotten to an instrumental part, and Oz backed away from the mic and leaned over to Devon. "Hey. That girl. Who is she?"

"She's an exchange student. I think she's from South America."

Oz shook his head. "No, not her. The eskimo."

Devon shrugged.

*Who is that girl?*

The princess had never been so happy in her life. True, the music was a trifle strange, but she found she liked it. And ultimately, it didn't matter. The important thing was that she had Xander in her arms. She liked how it felt.

Her heart started racing as he leaned in for a kiss.

As she angled her head to accept the kiss, she saw her hands, currently resting on Xander's shoulders.

They were starting to wither.

*No!*

The Guardian's energy should have lasted for days, not hours. Something was wrong. *Maybe because the Guardian is not truly human.*

The reasons didn't matter. She had to get away from Xander before he saw.

Before he could kiss her, she broke the embrace and ran away.

She tried to keep her hands at her sides, counting on the poor lighting in this place to keep anyone from noticing.

Gazing quickly around the room, she saw a boy

sitting alone on the staircase. She didn't recognize the culture he was supposed to represent, nor did she much care. All that mattered was that he was alone and so would be easy prey.

It took only a few moments and a bright smile to lure the boy—Jonathan was his name—into the backstage area. She removed the straw hat he wore as part of his costume and started stroking his hair.

Jonathan was a bit nervous. "Your hands feel kinda—rough. Aren't you with Xander?"

In as seductive a voice as she could muster, the princess asked, "Does it look like I am with Xander?"

She leaned in to kiss him.

"Ampata!" called Xander's voice from nearby.

*No, my love,* the princess thought in anguish, *not now!*

However, the damage had been done. At the sound of his voice, Jonathan said, "That's my cue to leave," and dashed off.


After Ampata ran off the dance floor, Xander stared after her, completely confused.

"Okay, at least I can rule out something I said," he muttered. They hadn't said a word since they started dancing.

Xander thought they hadn't needed to.

He went after her, but couldn't see her in the crowd. He did pass by Willow, though, who hadn't moved. "Have you seen Ampata?"

Willow made an odd sort of motion.

Frowning, Xander asked, "What was that?"

"I shrugged."

*Note to self,* Xander thought, *shrugs and eskimo*

*parkas don't mix.* "Next time you should probably say, 'shrug,'" Xander said, then went off.

As he did so, he heard Willow say, "Sigh."

Working his way through the crowd, Xander caught sight of one of Cordelia's legion of followers dressed as a medieval Japanese woman. She was talking with Sven, the Swedish student who was staying at the Chase house.

"I thought this exchange student thing would be a great deal," Sven was saying, "but look what I got stuck with. 'Momento'? 'Punchy fruity drinky'? Is Cordelia even from this country?"

Under any other circumstances, Xander would have relished overhearing this. As it was, he filed it away for future abusing-Cordy purposes.

Now, though, he had to find Ampata. For the first time in a life filled with rejection, things were actually going well between Xander and a girl. He was damned if he was going to let this one go without the biggest fight of his life.

He went to the back hallway, calling out Ampata's name.

After a minute, he found her. She seemed somewhat out of sorts. "There you are. Why'd you run away?"

"Because—" Her voice broke. "I do not deserve you."

Xander gasped. "You think you don't deserve *me?*" He laughed. "Man, I *love* you."

So caught up was he in amazement that a girl would actually think she didn't deserve him that it took him a moment to realize what he had said.

Ampata turned away. Tears poured down her cheeks.

"Are those tears of joy? Pain? Revulsion?"

"I am very happy. And very sad."

She only sounded sad. "Then talk to me," Xander said. "Let me know what's wrong."

"I can't," she said, and fell into his arms, crying into his shoulders.

"I know why you can't tell me. It's a secret, right?"

She looked up at him and nodded.

"And if you told me, you'd have to kill me?"

She started crying again.

*Nice work there, Levity Boy.* "Oh, that was a bad joke. The delivery was off, too, I'm sorry, I—"

He stopped himself as he looked into her eyes.

Her eyes looked back.

Right now, he wanted nothing more in the world than to kiss Ampata. And he was fairly sure she wanted the same thing.

They kissed.

It was an amazing kiss.

Then Xander felt like the life was being sucked out of him, and the kiss suddenly became somewhat less amazing . . .

# CHAPTER 7

Buffy had been worried when the doorbell rang. She thought it might be Willow deciding to bag the dance and come over to Buffy's to mope over Xander.

She was rather confused to see Giles on the other side of the door.

"Thank heavens you're home," he said and barreled right on in.

As she closed the door behind him, she said, "Yup. Not at the dance. Not with my friends. Not with a life." Giles seemed unmoved by this attempt at guilt, so she moved on. "What are you doing here? I thought we were going to meet at the museum to find the bodyguard."

"No, he's already been found in the school restroom—mummified."

Buffy frowned. "Okay, I don't get it. Why would the mummy kill her own bodyguard?"

"Well, I've cross-referenced and I've looked at the pictograms anew. He was a guard all right, but it was his job to ensure that the mummy didn't awaken and escape."

"So Ampata translated wrong?" *Makes sense,* Buffy thought. *She's just a kid after all.*

*And yet . . .*

"Perhaps," Giles said.

"Hang on a sec. She was wiggy about the seal from minute one."

"Yes, I suppose she was," Giles agreed.

"Her trunks," Buffy said, and ran upstairs.

Following, Giles said, "I beg your pardon?"

"There was something weird about her luggage," Buffy said as she went into her room. The suitcase and two trunks were present. Buffy noticed that Ampata had put a padlock on one of the trunks—the one Buffy had been about to open when Xander arrived. "Take a look at the clothes," she said to Giles.

The Watcher looked through the luggage a bit hesitantly at first, until he realized that all the clothes were of the male variety. "These are certainly all boys' clothes. Why would a girl pack these?"

Buffy knelt down at the second trunk, broke off the lock with a flick of the wrist, and opened it.

She got a whiff of staleness. And decay. Not surprising, really, considering that the trunk contained a mummified corpse. *Latest in a series, collect 'em all.*

"How about this one? What kind of girl travels with a mummified corpse and doesn't even pack lipstick?"

Giles breathed out slowly. "Obviously, Ampata is our mummy."

"And our murderer. Giles, she's at the dance with Xander!"

Nodding, Giles said, "We need to get to the Bronze posthaste."

They ran downstairs and out to Giles's car. Buffy climbed into the passenger seat as Giles got in on the driver's side. It took three tries for the car to start, and then it inched along down the road.

Buffy groaned. She could've walked faster. "Come on—can't you put your foot down?"

"It *is* down," Giles said testily.

"One of these days, you're gonna have to get a grown-up car."

Giles just gave her another one of his looks.

Looking ahead through the windshield, Buffy said, "I should've guessed. Remember? Ampata wanted us to hide the seal."

Giles nodded. "And then she wanted us to destroy it, because—wait."

After a moment, Buffy prompted, "Waiting."

"Well, we already know that the seal was used to contain the mummy. If breaking it freed her—"

"Reassembling it will trap her," Buffy finished. *That's two plans in one day. Not bad for a stuffy old Brit and a perky young Slayer.*

"I'll go to the museum," Giles said, making a turn that would finally get them to the Bronze. "I'll drop you off, then I'll try to piece together the fragments there."

Nodding, Buffy said, "Okay. I'll get Xander before he gets smoothchie with Mummy Dearest."

Buffy didn't even wait for the car to stop before she leaped out, slamming the door shut behind her. Giles drove off toward the museum.

She wasted a full minute explaining to Dave the bouncer why she didn't have a costume. It seemed that the house rules for the evening were that no one was to be let in unless they represented a particular culture. Eventually, she convinced Dave that she was dressed as a Canadian farmer, and he let her in.

Making a mental note to strangle Dave once the crisis was past, she plowed her way through an international smorgasbord of teenagers. She didn't see Xander or Ampata, but she did eventually see Willow wearing, of all things, an eskimo suit.

"Where's Xander?"

"He's looking for Ampata."

"We need to find them. Ampata is the mummy."

Willow's eyes widened. "Oh." Then she smiled with a viciousness Buffy wouldn't have expected from her. "Good." Then her face fell in much more Willowlike horror. "Xander!"

"Where'd they go?"

"Backstage, I think," Willow said as the two of them moved off in that direction.

Xander's experiences with kisses were appallingly limited, but even so, he was pretty sure that this was intense as it got. It really did feel like the life was being sucked out of him.

Then, again, Ampata broke it off. "No!" she cried. "I can't!"

Xander fell to the floor, completely drained. He'd

heard about kisses that could take your breath away, but this was ridiculous.

Ampata knelt down beside him. "Xander, I am so sorry."

He wanted to ask her what she was sorry for, but he couldn't work up the energy to form the words.

Suddenly, she stood up and put her hands to her head. "The seal," she said through clenched teeth, like she was in pain or something.

Then she ran off.

"Ampata . . ." Xander croaked. Then he just lay there. His strength started to come back to him. Slowly.

"Are you okay?"

The voice startled him. He looked up to see Buffy, still in her overalls, and Willow, still in her eskimo suit. *I thought Buffy was going to the museum with Giles. . . .*

"I think so," he said slowly in answer to the question. "Boy, that was some kiss."

"Where's Ampata?"

Xander had just been about to ask the same question. He tried to bring his thoughts into focus. "She said something about the seal."

Buffy stood up. "The seal. Giles. Come on!"

The conversation was making less and less sense. "What's going on?"

"He doesn't know," Willow said.

*Doesn't know what?* he thought.

"We'll tell him on the way," Buffy said as she and Willow helped him up and back out into the main part of the Bronze.

\* \* \* \*

The princess had sworn she would never come back to this hated place, but she found herself once again at the Treasures of South America exhibit.

When that idiot boy with the braces had broken the seal, she at last attained freedom after five centuries of dying hell. No matter what, she could not allow the seal to be repaired. She would never go back to her former existence. She had a reason to live now.

She had Xander. And she would let nothing take him away from her.

As she approached the exhibit, she heard a familiar voice. "'Inca cosmology unites the Bird-Head with its paler twin.'" A pause, then: "Oh, yes—its paler twin."

It was that archivist, Giles. He was obviously attempting to patch the Seal. *Damn him!* He reminded her of the high priest. So smug, so superior. Always telling her how noble it was for her to die for Sebancaya. *As if he had any idea what it was he asked of me. As if this fool has any idea what he is condemning me to.*

She saw him now, kneeling by her tomb. He was reading from one of his texts. "'The Condor soars, but the prey is in his talons.' That's it."

He then started piecing more of the seal together. The princess could feel its power calling to her.

*No!*

Her arms and legs had completely withered. Soon her entire body would decay, and then she would be helpless. She summoned her strength and moved to the dais.

"'The spondylus shell evokes Mamacocha, Mother of All the Water.' Well, that's it. Just one more piece."

Reaching with a gnarled hand, she tore the seal from the archivist's grasp and hurled it away. It shattered, its hold on her broken forever.

With her other hand, she grabbed the archivist by the throat and squeezed. She did not kill him, however. He could not be drained if he was dead.

As she leaned in for the kiss, a voice sounded from behind and below her. "I'll say one thing for you Incan mummies, you don't kiss and tell."

The princess whirled around to see Buffy standing at the entrance. The American girl then leaped up to the platform on which the sarcophagus sat, and landed in a fighting position. The princess was surprised. Buffy had shown no such abilities before.

Dropping the archivist's unconscious form into the tomb, the princess said, "Looks like you've been keeping some secrets from me. You're not a normal girl."

Buffy snorted. "Oh, and you are?" And then she whirled and kicked at the princess twice, then followed it with a punch.

Anyone else would have been felled by these blows, but the princess was stronger than that, even in her weakened state. She grabbed Buffy's wrist in mid-punch and flipped her around to the edge of the sarcophagus.

*The girl is powerful. She should last me for days,* the princess thought as she leaned in to kiss Buffy.

But Buffy was more difficult prey than the archivist. She head-butted the princess, sending her reeling. Buffy followed that with another kick, which the princess ducked.

Buffy charged, and again the princess was able to

turn her attack against her and toss her into the sarcophagus. Then she closed the lid.

She and the archivist would keep. The princess needed to feed before she could take Buffy on again. She could feel the strength flowing out of her. She had to find another victim.

Turning a corner, she crashed into Willow, no longer wearing the outfit of the people to the north. Forcing her weakening fingers to work, she clasped one hand around a now-terrified Willow's throat. "This won't hurt."

"Let her go!" said the voice the princess did not want to hear.

She turned to see Xander. *No, my love, please, I did not want you to see me like this!*

"If you're gonna kiss anybody, it should be me," Xander said.

The princess could feel the tears welling in her eyes. "Xander, we can be together, just let me have this one."

"That's *never* gonna happen."

The feeling was leaving her arms and legs. Soon they would be useless unless she could feed.

"I must do it," she said urgently. "I must do it now, or it is the end. For me and for us." She moved in on Willow.

"No!" Xander cried, and leaped between them, throwing Willow aside. The princess did not have the arm strength to resist. The weakness had crept up to her torso now. She barely had the ability to put her hands on Xander's shoulders.

He looked into her eyes. Those same eyes that gazed upon her with love less than an hour ago now stared at her with anger. "You want life, you're gonna have to take mine. Can you do that?"

Fear gripped the princess. The seal had kept her preserved, but she had destroyed the seal and killed the Guardian. The instruments of the curse were removed, and the only pracitioners of Sebancaya's will were centuries dead.

If she died now, she would die forever.

She could not face that. She had finally tasted life, and she would not, *could* not let it go.

Not even for Xander.

"Yes," she said hungrily, leaning in with the last of her strength to kiss him for one final time.

Then she heard the sound of the sarcophagus lid being thrown to the floor. Out of the corner of her eye, she saw Buffy leaping toward her.

The princess no longer had even the strength to turn her head to face Buffy.

Buffy grabbed her by the shoulders and tore her away from Xander.

The last thing the princess saw were her arms, which had been ripped from their sockets, still clinging to dear, sweet Xander.

The last thing she felt was the impact against the floor.

Then, oblivion.

Xander hadn't slept well that night. The rather gross image of Ampata's disembodied arms still clinging to his shoulders even as the rest of her shattered into a thousand pieces after Buffy threw her to the floor simply wouldn't go away.

The next morning, he and Buffy walked through the quad before homeroom. Buffy was sipping on a soda. She silently offered him a sip, which he just as silently declined.

Xander's great desire to not talk warred with his instinctive need to constantly talk, and the latter finally won out. "I'm really the Fun Talking Guy today, huh? Sorry."

"That's okay," Buffy said. "We don't have to talk."

Sighing, Xander said, "I just—" He cut himself off, not sure if he should say what he wanted to say. Then, *Why not? What do I have to lose?*

"Present company excluded," he said, "I have the worst taste in women of anyone in the world, ever."

"Ampata wasn't evil," Buffy said. "At least not to begin with. And I do think she cared about you."

"Yeah, but I think the whole sucking-the-life-out-of-people thing would've been a strain on the relationship."

He thought about the real Ampata Gutierrez, whose no doubt anticipated trip to America ended in a smelly bus depot at the hands of a long-dead mummy. He thought about the bodyguard, who simply tried to do his job. He even thought about Rodney Munson, who had been Scuzzy Punk Poster Boy for ten years running. None of them, not even Rodney, deserved what happened to them.

"She was gyped," Buffy then said. "She was just a girl and she had her life taken away from her. I remember how I felt when I heard the prophecy that I was gonna die. I wasn't exactly obsessed with doing the right thing."

"Yeah, but you did. You gave up your life."

Buffy smiled. "I had you to bring me back."

Xander returned the smile. Maybe nothing would come of his feelings for Buffy, but right now, he could deal with that. It was worth it, for the moment, just to have her there.

They continued walking in companionable silence.

# TONIGHT, PART 3

In retrospect, of course, those were innocent times—at least by comparison. After all, Angel and Buffy seemed to be doing well, as did Giles and Ms. Calendar. Willow even found someone: Oz, the guitar player from Dingoes Ate My Baby.

Xander had been more than a little dubious about Oz. Sure, he took a bullet for Willow when one of the Tarakan assassins shot at Buffy in a crowded hallway, but still, Xander had been concerned. However, when Oz learned the truth about Sunnydale—after Buffy staked a vampire right in front of him—he seemed fairly mellow about it.

And then, of course, there was the fact that Oz was a werewolf . . .

However, the arrival of those Tarakan assassins led to another significant change in Xander's life.

It all started when Xander and Cordelia had gone to Buffy's place early one morning. The Slayer had gone missing and not checked in. Spike and Drusilla had hired the Tarakan assassins, three supernatural bounty hunters. Buffy and Angel had taken care of one, and then Buffy had disappeared. They would later learn that Angel had been kidnapped by Spike and Dru, and Buffy had taken refuge from the assassins in Angel's apartment.

While Xander searched the empty house, Cordelia let in a door-to-door makeup salesman. Unfortunately, he turned out to be one of the assassins: a creature made entirely out of worms.

The pair of them managed to hide in the basement, duct-taping the door shut to keep the worms out.

Stuck in a basement with Cordelia Chase would never have been at the top of Xander's list of favorite things to do. Cordelia apparently felt the same way. They spent the entire time arguing.

"I can't believe I'm stuck here spending what are probably my last moments on earth with *you!*" Cordelia had said.

"I *hope* these are my last moments! Three more seconds of you, and I'm gonna—"

"You're gonna what? Coward!"

"Moron!"

"I hate you!"

"I hate *you!*"

Over twelve years, Xander and Cordelia had played plenty of scenes with this dialogue, but never before with this passion. Their arguing had always been of the dry-zinger variety—an insult here, a tossed-off witticism there.

This was the first time there was any major emotion in it.

After exchanging vows of undying hatred with Cordelia, Xander's blood was rushing, his heart was pounding, and he was filled with a deep, powerful, intellectual loathing—

And a much deeper, much more powerful urge to kiss her.

He reached for her just as she reached for him.

Unlike his kiss with Ampata, which was draining, this kiss with Cordelia seemed to feed on itself and grow more intense with each passing second. It was as if they'd both taken the vitriol and frustration they'd built up over their time trapped in the basement and thrown it all into one spit-swap.

After a dozen eternities, they broke the kiss.

"We *so* need to get out of here," Xander said emphatically, and Cordelia heartily agreed.

They managed to escape thanks to some quick thinking and liberal use of a garden hose. Eventually, the Tarakan assassins were dispatched, Angel was rescued, and Spike and Drusilla got a large church organ dropped on their heads. All in all, a happy ending.

Except for this one niggling problem. Cordy and Xander both agreed that what happened in the basement was a mistake. They did not agree on whose fault it was. In fact, they argued over that very subject for almost a full minute—right up until the point where they started kissing again.

The second time was even more passionate than the first.

Their relationship, such as it was, started out purely

physical. Periodically, they would sneak into a broom closet and neck. Making the relationship public was out of the question. Cordelia dated jocks and lead singers of bands; Xander had spent his life considering Cordy's social circle to be Public Enemy Numbers One through Ten. Neither could stand the humiliation. Besides, just because they made out didn't mean they *liked* each other or anything . . .

Around Buffy's seventeenth birthday, it did come out, however. Willow, to put it mildly, did not take it well. ("It's against all laws of God and man!" was her exact comment.)

Unknowingly breaking the curse on his soul, Angel reverted to his old, demonic self and joined Spike and Dru in their quest to wipe out humanity. Angel was now a full-fledged bad guy. Worse, the source of all their info on the curse was Ms. Calendar. It turned out that she had been sent to Sunnydale by the Romany elders to keep an eye on Angel. This little revelation put something of a strain on the Giles/Calendar coupling.

With all that, going public with his and Cordy's relationship didn't seem like such a major thing.

*Emphasis,* he thought, *on the word "seem"* . . .

# BEWITCHED, BOTHERED, AND BEWILDERED

## MID-JUNIOR YEAR

# CHAPTER 1

The lawyer was found dead with puncture marks in his neck and blood in his mouth. Buffy had tracked down and staked the vampire responsible for the murder. However, the blood in the mouth meant there may have been a sucking thing going on instead of just a feeding. So, the night after the lawyer's funeral, Buffy's patrolling consisted of waiting by the graveside in case the lawyer came back as a newly minted member of the Sunnydale Fang Club.

Since this was fairly boring work, Xander offered to keep her company while she waited. Besides, he needed a consultation from a teenage girl. Usually, he'd go to Willow, but since this involved his love life, he thought it would be kinder to talk to Buffy.

After spending ten minutes making lame jokes about the lack of difference between vampires and lawyers, Buffy finally said, "Xander, you've been not telling me something since we got here." She was sitting on the headstone opposite the lawyer's while Xander paced back and forth.

"Sorry." He reached into his pocket and pulled out the little box from the jewelry store. He opened it and removed the necklace.

It was silver, with a solid silver heart dangling from it. Xander had originally been saving up to buy a snazzy new skateboard. But he hadn't actually gone 'boarding in almost a year. Besides which, it was February, which meant Valentine's Day.

For the first time in his life, Xander actually had someone to give a gift to on that day. Hence the trip to Grossman's Jewelers and the spending of the skateboard money on the necklace.

"So what do you think?" he asked nervously.

"It's nice," Buffy said.

"But do you think Cordelia will like it?"

"I don't know." Buffy pointed at the heart. "Does she know what one of these is?"

Xander laughed. "Okay, big yuks. When are you guys gonna stop making fun of me for dating Cordelia?"

"I'm sorry," Buffy said, sounding like she meant it. "But never," she added, sounding like she meant it a lot more. "I just think you could find someone more—" she hesitated, "better."

Xander snorted. "Parallel universe, maybe. Here, the only other person I'm interested in is, um, unavailable."

The look on Buffy's face showed that she knew who

he meant, saving him the embarrassment of saying it out loud.

"Besides," he continued, "Cordy and I are really getting along. We're not fighting as much, and yesterday we just sat together, not even speaking. You know, just enjoying comfortable silence." He thought back over that, and added, "Man, that was dull."

"I'm glad that you guys are getting along," Buffy said with a smile. "Almost really. And don't stress over the gift."

"Well, this is new territory for me. I mean, my Valentines are usually met with heartfelt restraining orders."

"She'll love it."

Xander started pacing again. "I wish dating was like Slaying—y'know, simple, direct. Stake to the heart, no muss, no fuss."

The lawyer chose that moment to climb up out of the grave and embrace his new lease on unlife.

Despite expecting a man in a suit and fangs to come up through the dirt, Xander was still caught off-guard, and fell to the ground in shock. *Oh, God, I'm gonna die.*

Buffy, however, came to the rescue, as usual. She leaped off the gravestone, grabbed the vamp from behind, and threw him to the ground. As he got up, Buffy gave him a double kick, then punched him four times.

Xander had to admit, he loved watching Buffy in action. No matter how many times he saw her kick butt, he never got tired of it.

This particular vampire, however, had an especially

resilient butt. He stood up to her punches, then grabbed her and threw her at the wall of a nearby mausoleum. Buffy took less than a second to recover, give the vamp a low kick to the ankle, then a leaping kick to the throat.

That sent the undead lawyer sprawling on the grass and dirt. As he tried to get up, Buffy reached into her jacket, pulled out a stake, and slammed it into the guy's heart.

*Scratch one undead member of the legal profession,* Xander thought as the vampire collapsed into dust. *If that isn't a redundancy or anything.*

Buffy reached out to help Xander up. "Sorry to say, Xand, Slaying is a tad more perilous than dating."

Smiling, Xander said, "Well, you're obviously not dating Cordelia."

Valentine's Day in Sunnydale, and Cordelia Chase was concerned.

Nobody called her back last night. They had major outfit coordinating to take care of for tonight's dance. If they weren't careful, there might be some serious fashion overlap—or worse, someone could be dressing in something old. Katie in particular had a tendency to wear last month's clothes. Cordelia had been trying to break her of the habit, but it was slow going.

Cordelia had just purchased a gorgeous new red linen minidress, and so she needed to get Dori to switch to a different outfit. Dori could always wear that red silk sleeveless dress to the pledge dance, or something.

She saw Harmony, Laura, Kimberley, and Dori all sitting around at one of the walls.

But as Cordelia started walking toward them, they got up and headed into the school. *Didn't they see me?*

"Wait up," she called out to them, and walked faster across the quad so she could catch up. But they didn't stop. "Hey, wait up!" she said, louder. When she finally reached them, she said tersely, "Excuse me? Where's the fire sale?"

The four of them stopped and turned around. "Oh, sorry," Harmony said. "Didn't see you."

Cordelia could've sworn they'd looked right at her just before they got up, but she decided she had been imagining it.

"Well, why didn't you call me back last night? We need to talk about our outfits for the dance. I'm going to wear red and black," she looked pointedly at Dori, "so you need to switch."

"Red and black?" Kimberley interrupted. "Is that what Xander likes?"

"Xander?" Cordelia asked. "What does he have to do with this?" Fashion consultation was, after all, girls' work. Boys—least of all Xander, the terminally fashion impaired—didn't enter into it.

Harmony said, "Well, a girl wants to look good for her geek."

They all giggled at that. Giggled! Cordelia couldn't believe it. "Xander is just—"

Harmony interrupted. "When are you two gonna start wearing cute little matching outfits? 'Cause I'm planning to vomit." She looked at the other three. "Let's go."

They all walked off, leaving Cordelia with her mouth hanging open.

She was stunned. First she's interrupted—twice!—and then she's walked out on.

*What is their deal?*

Then she sighed. *Their deal is my loser boyfriend. And if one of them started dating Xander, would I be acting any different?*

As the bell rang in English class, Ms. Beakman said, "Papers on my desk. Anybody tries to leave without giving me a paper is looking at a failing grade." The paper was instead of a midterm. You had to write an essay on one of five novels. Xander had gone for *Great Expectations,* a book he found barely readable. The recent movie version was a lot easier to get through, but that was mainly because it had Gwyneth Paltrow in it.

It had taken all night, but Xander had somehow managed to squeeze a six-page paper out of the inanity of Charles Dickens's alleged classic. "Ha ha ha," he muttered as others in the class got up and handed their papers in, "this time I'm ready for you. No F for Xander today. No, this baby's my ticket to a sweet D-minus."

As Xander gathered his books into his backpack, he noticed Willow saying hi to Amy Madison. "Hey, Amy."

"Hey," the thin blonde said in reply. "You guys going to the Valentine's Day Dance at the Bronze? I think it's gonna be a lot of fun."

Willow looked like she was about to burst. *Here she goes again,* Xander thought.

"Go ahead," Buffy said, "you know you want to say it."

"My boyfriend's in the band!" Willow squealed.

*Assuming he's had his paper training,* Xander thought, perhaps a little cruelly. Xander mostly liked Oz, but he had a problem with Willow dating a guy who turned into a slavering beast three nights a month.

*Then again, in this town, that makes him pretty standard dating material . . .*

"Cool," Amy said in response to Willow, laughing.

"I think you've now told everybody," Buffy said.

Willow grinned. "Only in this hemisphere." Xander rolled his eyes. This was a level of goofiness that Willow usually only achieved when computer software was involved.

"What about you?" Amy asked Buffy.

"Oh, Valentine's Day is just a cute gimmick to sell cards and chocolate."

Amy nodded. "Bad breakup, huh?"

"Believe me when I say, 'uh-huh.'"

Buffy and Willow handed in their papers to Ms. Beakman just as Xander got up from his chair. As they walked out, Amy approached the teacher and looked right at her.

Ms. Beakman looked blankly ahead for a minute, then proceeded to mime receiving a paper. "Thank you, Amy," she said.

Amy then smiled and left.

*What just happened here?* Xander thought.

Then he remembered Amy's mother.

Catherine Madison had been the Sunnydale High School cheerleading champion some twenty years back. Her trophy still had a place of honor in the display case outside the library. When her daughter refused to follow in Mommy Dearest's footsteps, Catherine decided to dabble in the occult. She found several spells, including one that would switch her body with her daughter's so she could relive her glory days as a Sunnydale High cheerleader.

In order to make the squad, Catherine had done some serious damage, causing one girl to spontaneously combust, sealing another's mouth shut, striking Cordelia blind, and hitting Buffy with some kind of whammy that almost killed her. Giles managed to reverse the body-switching spell, and Buffy had used a mirror to reverse one of Catherine's magic attacks.

No one knew what became of Catherine after that. Amy went to live with her father and stepmother, and seemed happy to stay far away from Mom's old vocation.

*Looks like she had a thing for Mom's other hobby, though,* Xander thought as he handed his own paper to Ms. Beakman, then ran to catch up with Willow and Buffy.

"I just hate to think of you solo on Valentine's Day," Will was saying as Xander came up behind them.

"I'll be fine," Buffy said. "Mom and I are gonna have a pig-out and vidfest. It's a time-honored tradition among the loveless."

Xander asked, "Did you guys see that?"

"See what?" Buffy asked in reply.

"In class. I think Amy just worked some magic on Ms. Beakman."

Buffy frowned. "You mean like witchcraft?"

"Y'know, her mom's a witch," Willow said, her thoughts tracking with Xander's.

"And an amateur psycho," Buffy said, showing that her thoughts tracked with Xander's also. "Amy's the last person that should be messing with that stuff."

Xander started, "Maybe I should go talk to—"

He was interrupted by a British voice calling out, "Buffy!" He looked up to see Giles approaching. Just for something different, he was wearing tweed. "Buffy, can I have a word?"

Buffy shrugged. "Have a sentence, even."

"Oh, good," Giles said, taking a minute to get the joke. "Well . . ."

Giles trailed off. The Watcher was staring at a point behind the trio. Xander turned to see Ms. Calendar walking out of her computer class, talking to one of the students.

Then she turned and saw the four of them.

The temperature in the area seemed to Xander to drop about thirty degrees, the cold radiating from Buffy, whose entire body tensed up.

After an awkward silence, Ms. Calendar said, "Rupert."

"Ms. Calendar," Giles said tersely in reply.

Another awkward silence. Xander shifted from foot to foot, wanting to be anywhere but here. Ever since Jenny Calendar's involvement in Angel's curse had been revealed—even if only as a bystander—the Slayer and her Watcher had turned a united back on the techno-pagan. It had brought her growing romance with Giles to a grinding halt.

"I'm glad we ran into each other actually," Ms. Calendar finally said, nervously twirling her raven-black hair. "I was hoping we could, uh . . . You have a minute?"

"Uh, actually, not just now," Giles replied coolly. "I have a matter I must discuss with Buffy."

Buffy finally turned to look at Ms. Calendar. *If looks could kill,* Xander thought, *there'd be the corpse of a computer science teacher in front of us.*

"Right," the Slayer said coldly. "Let's go."

Giles and Buffy walked off.

Xander had never really understood what the phrase *tension so thick you could cut it with a knife* meant until this particular moment.

Ms. Calendar glanced at both Xander and Willow, looking pained. Willow looked stricken. Xander had no idea how he himself looked.

Finally, the computer-teacher-cum-Gypsy walked off, the *clack clack* of her heels sounding unusually loud against the linoleum floor.

Xander let out the breath he hadn't realized he'd been holding. *Well, that was fun.* Xander was of the opinion that Buffy was way overreacting to Ms. Calendar. Yes, she had lied to them, though was it was more a lie of omission. But Buffy seemed to be holding Ms. Calendar responsible for what happened to Angel. To Xander's way of thinking, that fell square into the category of misdirected aggression.

Besides, with Angel having gone to the other side, they needed all the allies they could get. Alienating someone with Ms. Calendar's magical talents wasn't practical.

*But who's thinking practical? What's Willow's line—"Love makes you do the whacky"?*

Sighing, he and Willow went off to their next class in silence.

Giles led a very stiff Buffy into the library. His own emotions were whirling like a dervish, but he kept them under control. That was his job, after all: to keep his own emotions in check as he supported the Slayer.

Right now, the Slayer wanted nothing to do with Jenny Calendar. Whether or not Giles agreed with her sentiments was irrelevant. How Giles felt about Jenny was even less relevant. He was the Watcher. He had a duty.

And he had the tattoo of a mystic sigil on his left arm as a constant reminder of what happened the last time he shirked his duty.

"Are you okay?" Buffy asked.

Giles almost laughed, but it would've been a bitter one. "Me? I'll be fine," he lied. He forced his thoughts back to his reasons for summoning Buffy in the first place. "I'm a little more concerned about you, actually. Since Angel, um—*turned,* I've been reading up on his earlier activities. Feeding patterns, and the like." He hesitated.

"And?" Buffy prompted.

"Around Valentine's Day, he's rather prone to brutal displays of—what he would think of as affection."

"Like what?"

Images of brutalized pets and severed limbs floated into his head, and he decided to spare the Slayer the specifics. "No—no need to go into detail."

"That bad?"

"Suffice it to say, I think it would be best if you stayed off the streets for a few nights. I'll patrol, keep my eye on things. Better safe than sorry."

Buffy let out a long breath. "It's a little late for both."

Giles couldn't think of anything to say in response to that.

# CHAPTER 2

The vampire named William—sometimes called "the Bloody," most often called Spike—didn't go for the gift-giving sentiment as a rule. Valentine's Day, though, was different, especially this year, for two reasons. For one thing, Spike had always liked the idea of celebrating the anniversary of one of history's more entertaining massacres.

For another, given his physical condition, gifts were all he could give to Drusilla.

It was maddening, really. Spike had only come to Sunnydale in the first place in order to find some way to cure Dru of her illness. While the physical wounds of the mob attack in Prague had healed, she was still drained, like a car with a low battery.

They had finally found a cure in the du Lac

manuscript, stolen from the Sunnydale High library. Though they hadn't completed the ritual laid out in the manuscript, they had done enough to restore Drusilla to her old self. But that thrice-damned Slayer put another one of her spanners into the works by dropping a church organ on him and leaving him to burn.

Spike had encountered many Slayers in almost two centuries. None of them had even so much as scratched him. He'd even killed two of them himself.

*Until this blond tart came 'round.*

Now, when Spike wanted nothing more than to put as much distance between him and Buffy as possible, he was stuck in a bloody wheelchair. He had burns over half his body, and his legs had been crushed. The damage would heal in due time, but he couldn't travel until then.

Worse, Angel had returned.

If one had asked Spike months ago, he would've cheered at the prospect of his sire returning to the fold. Now, though . . .

Drusilla opened the box that Spike had given her and stared in wide-eyed wonderment at the antique ruby necklace inside. The rubies were blood red, of course.

"Fancy it, pet?" he asked.

She sighed contentedly. "It's beautiful."

Spike smiled. He lived for these moments. "Nothing but the best for my gir—"

A wet *plop* sound interrupted him, as a human heart was placed on the table.

It was Angel. "Happy Valentine's Day, Dru."

"Oh!" Drusilla said with an even bigger sigh than Spike's necklace got. "Angel, it's still warm!"

Spike seethed. Angel had been doing this ever since he got back—doing everything he could to upstage Spike. Angel had sired both vampires, but he'd made Drusilla insane before turning her into a demon. As a result, he tended to be possessive of her. Much more possessive than Spike would've liked, really.

"I knew you'd like it," Angel said with a feral grin. "I found it in a quaint little shop girl." Angel noticed the necklace and picked it up. "Cute," he said dismissively, then moved to put the necklace on Dru. "Here."

Spike started to wheel over. "I'll get it," he said through clenched fangs.

"Done," Angel said, having clasped the necklace around her neck and shifted her hair over it. Was it Spike's imagination, or did Angel stroke her hair? "I know Dru gives you pity access," Angel continued, "but you have to admit, it's so much easier when I do things for her."

Resisting the urge to respond directly, Spike decided to instead—not for the first time—remind Angel of something he seemed to care much too little about. "You would do well to worry less about Dru and more about that Slayer you've been tramping around with."

Angel smiled fondly. "Dear Buffy. Hmm. I'm still trying to decide the best way to send my regards."

This was Angel's problem all over, Spike thought. Indeed, the problem with most vampires, at the end of the day. All caught up in rituals and ways of doing things and trying to be fanciful when they should just act and have done with it.

"Why don't you rip her lungs out? Might make an impression."

Angel shook his head. "It lacks poetry."

*Case in bloody point.* "It doesn't have to." Spike looked at Dru. "What rhymes with lungs?"

"Don't worry, Spike," Dru said with a distressingly fond gaze down at her blood-soaked gift. "Angel always knows what speaks to a girl's heart."

*That's what I'm worried about,* Spike thought.

Buffy had lost track of the amount of junk food she had eaten. She had considered keeping a tally, but by the time they got halfway through *War of the Roses*—the first of their double feature, which was followed by Buffy and her mom's favorite film, *Thelma and Louise*—she gave up.

As they got to the scene in *T&L* when Susan Sarandon and Geena Davis picked up a hitchhiking Brad Pitt, Mom said, "Pass me the Malomars."

Buffy didn't move. "I can't."

"Good," Mom said.

It worried Buffy how much the progress of Geena Davis's character in the movie paralleled Buffy's own life. A woman in a world she didn't know was so limiting, changed by violence into something greater than what she was.

A knock came from the door. Buffy handed the bowl of Thin Mints that she hadn't even realized was still in her lap to Mom and said, "Here." She hauled herself up off the couch and went to the front door.

There was nobody there.

Suddenly, all her senses went on alert. Pranksters like this were common in L.A., but in Sunnydale, the only people who went for the knock-on-the-door-and-run-away trick were demonic.

She closed and locked the door, then went back into the living room.

Her mother was gone. *Thelma and Louise* continued to play on the TV.

"Mom?"

She went into the kitchen, hoping that Mom just went for something to drink. She tried not to think about what Giles couldn't bring himself to tell her about Angel's Valentine's Day habits.

"Mom?"

Mom wasn't in the kitchen.

Then she heard the back door close.

She whirled around, startled.

There was Mom. She was holding a long, black box. "Buffy, it's me."

Buffy allowed herself to breathe again. "Yeah. You startled me a little."

"I was just checking the back door." She handed the box to Buffy. It looked like a flower box. "Somebody left these for you."

Opening the box slowly, Buffy saw a dozen red roses and a card. The card simply read, Soon. It also had a small drawing of a dead rose next to it.

*Oh my God.*

Xander sat in the Bronze, fidgeting nervously. Cordelia still hadn't shown up yet. They were originally going to come together, but Cordy had decided at the last minute to just meet here. So Xander sat next to

Willow, constantly taking the gift box out of his pocket, tossing it back and forth from hand to hand, then putting it back in his pocket, then taking it out a minute later.

Willow didn't even notice. She was listening to the music. Oz's band, Dingoes Ate My Baby, was playing a straight-out rock number. Xander had to admit, the band was good, and he *loved* their name. But just at the moment, he was way too nervous to appreciate them.

"Oz has his cool hair today," Willow said. Oz had been going back and forth between his natural strawberry blond hair color and jet black. No one was entirely sure why. "I think I'm a groupie," Willow added, earnestly.

Xander smiled at her. He had to admit that, even if he wasn't keen on Oz, he liked seeing Willow this happy.

*If only I could say the same about me. Where is Cordy?*

Finally, Cordelia entered. She looked around, seemed disheartened with something, then sat at a table by herself.

*Weird,* Xander thought as he gathered up his courage, went over the speech one last time, then went over to the table where Cordy sat.

As he approached, she got up.

Xander took a moment to take in her very hot minidress and how well she occupied it, then said, "Hey."

"Your clothes," she said, sounding almost stunned. "You look so good."

Xander was wearing a light gray button-down shirt,

black slacks, and a charcoal gray suit jacket. At least Buffy had said it was charcoal gray. Xander didn't see much difference between that and black, but he accepted that as secret girl knowledge and let it go. "I let Buffy dress me," Xander said, then at Cordy's look added quickly: "Well, not physically . . ."

"Perfect," Cordy said, sounding annoyed, of all things. "You had to make this harder didn't you?"

*I think I speak for everyone here when I say, "huh?"* Xander thought, recalling one of Buffy's lines to Giles. "Okay," he said slowly. "Clearly the fact that I please you visually has got us off on the wrong foot here."

"Xander—" she started.

"Let me finish," Xander said. He'd been rehearsing this speech since lunch, and he wasn't going to let her stop him now. He took a breath, then started. "I've been thinking a lot about us lately. The why and the wherefore. You know, once, twice, a kissy here, a kissy there. And you can chalk that all up to hormones. And maybe that's all we have here: tawdry teen lust. But maybe not. Maybe something in you sees something special inside me. And vice versa. I mean, I think I do. See something." *You're losing it,* he thought. *Cut to the chase, no pun intended.* "So . . ."

He handed her the gift box.

Cordelia opened it. "Xander, thank you." She took out the necklace. "It's beautiful." Then she lowered the chain into the box and said, "I want to break up."

Xander somehow managed not to scream. "Okay, not quite the reaction I was looking for."

"I know, I'm sorry," Cordy said, and for once in her life, she sounded sincere. "It's just—who are we kidding? Even if parts of us do see specialness—we don't fit."

A small part of Xander saw this coming. A lifetime of rejection, of guffawing from the female population, of overall abysmal luck in love had prepared him for this moment.

But not tonight. Of all nights, not tonight.

"Yeah, okay," he said, trying and failing to keep his temper. "You know what's a good day to break up with somebody? Any day besides Valentine's Day! I mean, what, were you just running low on dramatic irony?"

"I know, I didn't mean to do it this way," Cordy said, and again, she sounded sincere.

At another time, Xander would've been amazed at the genuineness of her emotions.

But, again, not tonight.

"Well, you did," Xander said, and turned on his heel and walked out of the Bronze.

*Well, at least things can't get any worse.*

# CHAPTER 3

**X**ander hadn't slept very well the previous night. Last year, when he'd asked Buffy to the prom, he'd said, "I don't handle rejection well. Funny, considering all the practice I've had." But no rejection had hurt quite like this one, because no other relationship had been even moderately successful. Even the thing with Ampata only lasted twenty-four hours before it literally disintegrated, and the other crushes never even got that far. This one, though, actually started to be something real.

So Xander went into class on the fifteenth of February thinking he was as low as he could possibly feel.

He hadn't taken into account the speed with which the high school gossip machine operated. Half the school was at the Bronze when the most popular girl

175

on campus dumped him, and the other half had heard about it from the first half by sunrise.

They giggled. They tittered. They guffawed. They pointed and laughed. They shook their heads in amused dismay. One jock, whom Xander didn't even know, said, "Dude, way to get dumped!"

Then he saw a lifeline: Buffy. *Finally, someone who'll understand.*

"Hey, Buffy, my bud, you would not believe the—"

"I can't talk right now," Buffy said urgently. "Angel."

Some might have viewed this as a bad thing, but right now what Xander needed was a distraction, even if it was the most extreme example of the psycho ex. "Need help?"

"It's all right," she said, and continued walking, probably heading to the library.

Xander sighed.

He moved on to see Cordy and four of her usual gaggle of bleached bimbos sitting on one of the benches outside the restrooms. Half the time Xander couldn't tell them apart. *Is that Harmony or Julianne next to her?* He then placed it as Harmony—she was a victim of that invisible girl last year.

Harmony was, in fact, the first one to speak. "Gee, Xander, maybe you should learn a second language so that even more girls can reject you."

They all laughed. Except Cordelia, who couldn't even make eye contact. Somehow, that just made it worse.

Xander walked off, then caught sight of a second lifeline.

Amy Madison.

In an instant, a plan began to form in Xander Harris's head. He thanked whatever gods or fates were responsible for his catching Amy's little illusion act on Ms. Beakman yesterday, and walked over to the young witchlet.

He grabbed Amy by the arm and led her to a corner.

"What are you doing?" she asked indignantly.

"Amy, good to see you," he said conversationally. Then, small talk taken care of, he said, "You're a witch."

"No, I'm not," she said with a forced laugh. "That was my mom, remember?"

"Yeah, I'm thinking it runs in the family. I saw you working that mojo on Ms. Beakman. Maybe I should go tell somebody about that."

*Okay, here's where we see if she calls my bluff.* The fact of the matter was, Xander didn't have a thing on her, not really. He had no proof, and it was unlikely that anyone, aside from Giles, would believe that a student had bewitched a teacher. But Xander was counting on the fact that Amy knew a, what Buffy could do; b, that Giles had reversed the body-switching spell Amy's mother had cast; and c, Xander was tight with both of them.

"Don't even—that is so mean!"

*Paydirt!* "Blackmail is such an ugly word."

Amy frowned. "I didn't say blackmail."

"Yeah, but I'm about to blackmail you, so I thought I'd bring it up."

"What do you want?" Amy said, defeated.

Xander laughed a bitter laugh. "What do I want? I want some respect around here. I want, for once, to come out ahead. I want the Hellmouth to be working for me. You and me, Amy, we're gonna cast a little spell."

"What kind?"

Several students walked in their direction, and Xander decided it was best to be discreet. He led Amy into an empty English classroom, closed the door, then said, "A love spell on Cordelia."

"A love spell?" she repeated.

"Yeah, y'know, just the basic, can't eat, can't sleep, can't breathe anything but little old *moi.*"

Amy shook her head. "That kind of thing is the hardest. I mean, to make someone love you for all eternity—"

"Whoa, whoa, back up. Who said anything about eternity? A man can only talk self-tanning lotion for so long before his head explodes."

Again, Amy frowned. "Well then, I don't get it. If you don't want to be with her forever, then what's the point?"

"The point is, I want her to want me. Desperately. So I can break up with her and subject her to the same hell she's been putting me through."

"Oh, I don't know, Xander," Amy said, wincing. "Intent has to be pure with love spells."

"Right. I intend revenge. Pure as the driven snow. Now, are you gonna play or do we need to have another chat about invisible homework?"

Sighing, Amy said, "I'll need something of hers. A personal object."

Xander smiled. He knew just the thing.

Buffy made a beeline for the library, where she saw Giles sitting and reading a book. *Big surprise, there.*

She walked right up to him and plopped the card from the flower box onto the book he was reading, startling him.

*Good. He deserves to be startled.* Buffy had tossed and turned all night, wondering what it was Giles hadn't told her about Angel. *He'd better damn well tell me now.*

" 'Soon' what, Giles? You never held out on me until the big, bad thing in the dark became my ex-honey."

"Where did this come from?" Giles asked.

"He said it with flowers. This isn't time to start becoming Mr. Protective Guy. I can't just hang around, and I can't prepare when I don't know what's coming."

Giles nodded. "Of course, you're right. Sit down."

Buffy sat as Giles got up to go into his office, probably to dig out some old Watcher diaries.

Cordelia was generally pretty happy with things. So far, today had been completely normal. She'd given Gwen advice on how to break up with John without jeopardizing her future on the pep squad. She'd convinced Dori not to wear that hideous butterfly pin, as only old people and last year's Dolce wearers wore butterflies. And they'd spent a good half hour talking about what a dork the guest lecturer for health class was.

The only exception had been the way everyone was laughing at Xander.

First of all, Cordelia Chase didn't need anyone to make fun of losers for her. Usually, the others followed her lead, they didn't try to take up the slack, like they were now. And she didn't see any need to hit Xander while he was down. It wasn't like with Mitch or Devon or any of the others, where they deserved ridicule after Cordelia broke it off. Unlike them, Xander *had* been paying sufficient attention to her.

It just didn't work out. One of those things that you realize and get on with your life.

Besides which, no one had ever giggled at Mitch or tittered at Devon.

Still, this was minor. In all other things, life was normal. She liked it.

Then she saw Xander walking toward her.

She started to go in the other direction, but Xander's big doofy legs worked in his favor, and he cut in front of her.

"Oh, c'mon, don't flatter yourself," Xander said coldly, "I'm not going to make a big scene. I just want the necklace back."

Cordelia's mouth fell open. "What? I thought it was a gift."

"No, last night it was a gift. Today, it's scrap metal. I figure I can melt it down. Sell it for fillings or something."

Aghast, Cordelia said, "You're pathetic." And she meant it. Maybe the others were right. How could he even *think* of taking the necklace back? Was he that petty? Just because the entire school was making fun of *him,* was that any reason to punish *her* by taking away her gift?

"C'mon," Xander said harshly, "I'm not going to add to the Cordelia Chase Cast-Off Collection."

That did it. She couldn't *believe* he was being so rotten. "It's in my locker," she said, stalling.

"I can wait."

Huffing, Cordelia went to her locker, and opened it all the way, blocking her from Xander's view.

As a general rule, Cordelia didn't wear button-down shirts. If she did, she did not button them all the way up to the neck. She had always been very proud of her clavicle, and saw no reason not to share it with the world. But today, she had put on a blue-and-white-striped shirt with a white collar and buttoned all the buttons.

It was the only way to wear the necklace without anyone seeing it.

She reached in under the collar and removed the hidden jewelry. She stared at the shiny silver heart.

Lots of guys had given her presents before. But, since they were from guys, they were generally ugly and/or useless. They were just to show that the guy in question was utterly devoted to her, which was all that mattered.

But this necklace was different. It was the most beautiful thing anyone had ever given her.

And she was furious that she had to give it back.

Slamming the locker shut, she stomped over to Xander and practically shoved the necklace into his hand. "Here. It's a good thing we broke up. Now I don't have to pretend I like it."

*Take that,* she thought.

If Xander was insulted, he didn't show it, the creep. He looked too angry. Cordelia had never seen him this angry before.

*Well, tough. If you're gonna toy with my feelings, you pay the price.*

They both stormed off in opposite directions, Cordelia never more sure that breaking up with that vindictive little geek was the right thing to do.

Xander had been hoping that Amy would just wave her magic wand over the necklace, say, "Bim sallah bim" or something, and that would be it.

No such luck.

They had gone after dark to one of the chem labs, where Amy had drawn the female symbol in red on the floor. Then she instructed Xander to take his shirt off. After he did so, she used the same red paint to draw three symbols on his chest. Amy called them sigils, and said they were mystic letters. Then she handed him a thick candle, told him to light it, then sit within the symbol, cross-legged, holding the lit candle over his lap.

The reason for being in a chem lab was simple. It was one of the few places in the school where you could boil things. Apparently, several rather pungent herbs needed to be boiled in water in order for this to work.

Xander sat in the middle of the female symbol, candle in hand, feeling very exposed without his shirt. He kept casting furtive glances at the candle, worried about where the wax might drip. That candle was now the only light source in the room.

Amy stood in front of the boiling water, clutching Cordelia's necklace, and reading from a book whose mustiness was enough to make Giles's books look shiny and new.

*"Diana, goddess of love and the hunt, I pray to thee. Let my cries bind the heart of Xander's beloved. May*

*she neither rest nor sleep—"* Amy dropped the necklace into the brew; a weird red smoke started shooting out of the beaker, providing another light source and casting sinister-looking shadows on her face, *"until she submits to his will only. Diana! Bring about this love and bless it!"*

Amy was shaking now, almost convulsing with, Xander assumed, mystical energy.

"Blow out the candle! Now!" she yelled.

He did so, and the room went dark.

"Great," Xander said after a moment. "Really. Good spell. Can I put my shirt on now?"

The next day, Xander went to school all prepared. Cordelia would profess her undying love for him. She would beg him to take her back.

And then he'd dump her.

He had an entire speech laid out. It had the one that went with the gift beat all to hell. It would be beautiful.

*But first things first,* Xander thought. *Gotta get the ball rolling.*

He found Cordelia sitting with a bunch of her lapdogs. He sauntered up to the little gathering and hovered near Cordelia.

*Any moment now, she'll be begging me to take her back.*

*Any moment now.*

*Okay, maybe now.*

Cordy continued gossiping, giving Xander the occasional sidelong glance, then finally snapping, "What?"

"Morning, ladies," he said with what he hoped was a seductive smile. "Some kinda weather we've been having, huh?"

"What do you want?" Cordelia asked. "You can't be sniffing around for more jewelry to melt, 'cause all you ever gave me was that Wal-Mart–looking thing."

Xander felt his crest falling. *She's not following the Love Potion #9 script.* He leaned in close to her. "Is this love? 'Cause maybe on you it doesn't look that different."

Cordelia could not *believe* that Xander was pulling this. She especially couldn't believe he was leaning into her personal space like that. Unless kissing was involved, she didn't even like that when they *were* dating, much less now.

Shoving him back, she asked, "What are you doing? Are you going, like, stalker-boy on me, now?"

"Sorry," Xander said, much more quietly this time. "My mistake."

"Yeah, I should say so."

With that, he went off.

Cordelia turned to Harmony. "What is his deal?"

Harmony, though, was looking at Xander as he went off with his tail between his gangly legs. "I know," she said. "Did he cut his hair or something? He looked halfway decent for a change."

Cordelia stared at Harmony in open-mouthed shock. "Halfway *what?*"

# CHAPTER 4

Xander wandered morosely into the library after classes ended. The day hadn't been quite as miserable as yesterday, but it still rated a 9.5 on the Life-Sucks-O-Meter. After going to all the trouble to blackmail Amy, after sitting shirtless on a cold lab floor with red paint on his chest and candle wax dripping into his nether regions, he got bupkuss.

The sole consolation was that the ridicule had lessened. *In fact,* he thought, *now that I think about it, it was just guys making fun of me today. The girls pretty much left me alone. What's up with that?*

Sighing to himself, he thought, *Well, at least things can't get any worse.*

"Ah, here's another," the Watcher was reading bits out of some book or other. "Valentine's Day, yes, Angel nails a puppy to the—"

"Skip it," Buffy said quickly.

"Yes, but—"

"I don't want to *know,*" Buffy said with feeling. "I don't have a *puppy.* Skip it."

"Right you are," Giles said, closing the book and getting up from the chair he had been sitting on the back of. "I'll get another batch."

As he went back to his office, Xander approached Buffy. "I have a plan. We use me as bait."

Buffy frowned. "You mean, make Angel come after you?"

"No, I mean chop me into little pieces and stick me on hooks for fish to nibble at, 'cause it would be more fun than *my* life."

"Yeah, I heard about you and Cordy. It's her loss."

Sighing, Xander said, "Not really the popular theory."

Buffy stood up and stared at Xander in a way she'd never stared at him before. "You know what I'd like? Why don't you and I go do something together tonight? Just the two of us."

"Really?" he said, surprised.

"Yeah. We can comfort each other."

Smiling, Xander asked, "Would lap dancing enter into that scenario at all? 'Cause I find that very comforting."

He had spoken facetiously. Xander spent most of his life speaking facetiously. It was how he dealt with reality.

So the last thing in the world he expected was a serious response.

Buffy actually leaned close to him and ran her fingers over his chest. "Play your cards right . . ."

*Somebody replaced Buffy with a pod person.* "Okay, you do know that I'm Xander, right?"

She leaned closer. "I don't know. I heard that you and Cordy broke up, and I guess I was surprised how glad I was. It's funny how you can see someone every day but not really *see* them, you know?"

*I've died and gone to heaven.* "Yeah, it's funny. And it's just getting funnier."

Buffy looked like she was about to say something else, but was interrupted by Amy walking in. She looked a tad nervous.

"Xander, can I talk to you for a minute?"

His first instinct was to tell her to get lost, but it was bad form to blow off someone who'd cast a love spell for you, even if she did get it wrong.

*And given the way Buffy's acting, maybe it's all for the best.*

"Yeah, okay," he said to the blond witch, then turned to the Slayer. "Hold that thought. Tightly."

Buffy smiled a seductive smile.

Xander followed Amy out of the library. As soon as the door closed, Amy said, "Xander, I don't think the spell worked out right."

"Oh yeah, it bombed. No biggie," Xander said dismissively. He stole a glance into the library to see Buffy staring right at him. Giles had come back in and was probably reciting another bit from Angel's Guide to Vampiric Stalking Techniques. But Buffy was obviously ignoring his every word.

"Well, we could always try again," Amy said. "I'm still pretty new at this."

"It's okay," Xander said, wanting this conversation to hurry up and end so he could get back to being with

Buffy. He wanted to spend as much time as he could with her now that she'd finally come to her senses. "You know what?" he said. "It was wrong to meddle with the forces of darkness. I see that now. I think we've all grown. I gotta go."

But Amy wasn't finished. "Well, we don't have to cast any spells. We can just hang out."

"Sure," Xander said, then realized what, exactly, Amy was saying. "What?"

"Well, I liked spending time with you. You're so sweet. Y'know, it's funny how you can see a person every day and—"

"Not really see them?" Xander finished. He felt all the blood drain from his face.

"Exactly!" Amy said with a smile.

Xander glanced into the library again. *Oh God.*

Amy and Buffy both had the exact same smiles on their faces.

*I should've known. Things aren't allowed to go right for me. There's a law, I'm sure of it. Thou shalt not kill, thou shalt not commit adultery, thou shalt not allow anything to go right for Xander Harris, for any reason, ever.*

"So anyway," Amy babbled on, "I thought it might be fun—"

"Hi, Xander?" someone interrupted.

Xander turned to see one of the Cordettes—Kimberley? no, it was Katie—staring at him. She had blond hair in a kind of U-shape style that was popular in the fifties and was coming back now for no good reason that Xander could see.

"What?" Xander asked, dazed.

"You're in Mr. Baird's history class, right? I thought maybe we could study together tonight."

Katie smiled the same smile as the other two. *This is bad.*

"Do you mind?" Amy asked snappishly. "We were talking."

Xander felt a sudden need to be far away from the female population of Sunnydale High. "I really gotta go right now," he said, quickly taking his leave of Amy and Katie.

As he worked his way out of the school, he noticed several other girls giving him that smile. Girls who would never have acknowledged his existence a week ago were now gazing at him seductively.

He arrived home to find the house empty, which wasn't unexpected. Neither Mom nor Dad was due home from work for a couple more hours. This meant that Xander could hide in the privacy of his own room and try to figure out how to clean up the latest mess he'd made of his life.

He closed the door, desperate to simply collapse on the bed and not think for a little while.

This plan was derailed by the body in the bed.

Life on the Hellmouth had given Xander's already fertile imagination plenty of ideas as to who or what could've been in his bed. As a result, it was almost a relief when it just turned out to be Willow hiding under the covers.

Almost.

Xander leaped from the bed in abject terror before Willow poked her head out.

"Sorry," she said. "I wanted to surprise you."

She didn't sound like Willow. She sounded like—
*Like Buffy, Amy, and Katie all did.*

"Good job," he said, feeling very much surprised. "High marks."

"Don't be so jumpy. I've been in your bed before."

"Yeah, but Will, we were both in footie pajamas."

Willow sat up, and Xander noticed that she was wearing one of his shirts. "Xand, I've been thinking," she started.

*Oh God, not the see-someone-every-day speech again.* "Will, I think I know what you've been thinking, but this is all my fault. I cast a spell and it sort of backfired."

"How long have we been friends?" Willow asked.

*Great, she hasn't heard a word I said.* "A long, long time. Too long to do anything that might change that now."

"Friendships change all the time. People grow apart. They grow *closer.*"

This didn't even sound like Willow. "This is good, how close we are now," Xander said quickly, hoping some of this would penetrate, knowing full well that it wouldn't. "I feel very comfortable with this amount of closeness. In fact, I could even back up a few paces and still be happy." He stepped backward to the door. "See?"

Willow got up out of the bed and walked toward him, then started unbuttoning the buttons on the shirt. Xander also couldn't help but notice that she wasn't wearing anything other than the shirt.

"I want you Xander, to be my first."

"Baseman? Please tell me we're talking baseball."

"Shhhh. We both know it's right," she said as she pinned him up against the door.

"It's not that I don't find you sexy—" Xander started.

"Is it Oz? Don't worry about him. He's sweet, but he's not you."

Xander clutched at that. "Yes he is! And you should go to him. 'Cause he's me."

Willow ignored that. Instead she nibbled Xander's ear.

*Okay, this is definitely not the real Willow.* This was a girl who thought playing "doctor" when they were kids involved medical texts.

He pushed her away and said, "That's it. This has gotta stop. It's time for me to act like a man. And hide."

With that, he dashed out the door.

Cordelia went to school on the morning of the seventeenth hoping for another ordinary day. Things had gotten so much better since she got over whatever virus she had that made her think dating Xander Harris was a *good* idea.

So she was more than a little taken aback when Harmony, Katie, Laura, and Dori all gave her the cold shoulder.

Assuming it to be some kind of practical joke, she said, "Ha. Very funny. What did I do now, wear red and purple together?"

"You know what you did," Harmony said, cold as an iced cappuccino. "Xander is wounded because of you."

They started to walk away. Cordelia stared after them. "Are you tripping? I thought you wanted me to break up with him."

"Only a sick pup would let Xander get away, no matter what her friends said."

With that, they all turned on their heels and walked off.

Cordelia couldn't believe it. *What does it take to make you people happy?* she cried.

# CHAPTER 5

If someone had told Xander that the most hellish day of his seventeen-year-old life would be the day that every girl in Sunnydale High School desperately wanted him, he'd have sent for the doctors in the white coats.

By now, he should have learned the universal truth of the phrase *be careful what you wish for, you might get it*. If nothing else, his "dream date" with that substitute teacher Ms. French should've driven that point home with large praying mantis–sized mandibles.

On this day, he got more propositions, expressions of devotion, and lines about how you see someone every day but don't really *see* them than he'd gotten in the previous seventeen years of life. *I've had more of that in any ten-minute* period *than in the last seven-teen years.*

Far worse, though, were the looks he was getting from the guys. A kind of *I'm going to kill you* look. The look Rodney Munson used to give him in class to let Xander know that his function after school would be to act as Rodney's punching bag.

By the end of the day, he couldn't take it anymore. He had tried to talk to Amy about reversing the spell, but she didn't pay attention to a word he said, preferring to carry on about Xander's eyes.

So he did the only thing he could do.

He ran to Giles.

"Xander, what is it?" the Watcher asked as Xander entered the library. He sounded concerned—obviously Xander's agitation was written all over his face.

"It's me. Throwing myself at your mercy."

"What? Why?"

Taking a deep breath, Xander said, "I made a mess, Giles. See, I found out that Amy's into witchcraft. And I was hurt, I guess, so I made her put the love whammy on Cordy. But it backfired. And now every woman in Sunnydale wants to make me her cuddle-monkey. Which may sound swell on paper, but—"

"Rupert, we need to talk," said a voice from behind Xander. He turned to see that Ms. Calendar had entered. "Hey, Xander," she said upon passing him. She turned to Giles, then turned back to Xander. "Nice shirt," she added, then turned back to Giles. "Look, Rupert, I know that you're angry at me, and I don't blame you. But I'm not just gonna go away. I mean, I care far too much about you to—" She cut herself off, then stared at Xander again. "Have you been working out?" She felt his bicep.

Xander indicated Ms. Calendar with his head and gave Giles a *see what I mean?* look.

Giles looked befuddled at first, but as soon as he saw Ms. Calendar go from her normal self to a fawning Xanderphile right in front of his eyes, he grew livid.

Yanking the computer teacher forcibly away from Xander's side, he said in a low, dangerous tone, "I cannot believe that you are fool enough to do something like this."

"Oh no," Xander said resignedly. "I'm *twice* the fool it takes to do something like this."

"Has, uh, has Amy tried to reverse the spell?"

"I get around Amy and all she wants to do is talk honeymoon plans."

"Rupert," Ms. Calendar said, "maybe I need to talk to Xander alone." She had That Smile on her face as she said it.

"Do you have any idea how serious this is?" Giles asked, again in the low tone. Xander would've preferred yelling, as this tone of voice was several orders of magnitude scarier. "People under a love spell are deadly. They lose all capacity for reason. And if what you say is true, and the entire female population is affected . . ." He trailed off, then said forcefully, *"Don't* leave the library. I'll find Amy and see if we can put a stop to this thing."

Giles moved to leave, stopped, grabbed Ms. Calendar, and dragged her off with him. She was very reluctant to go.

Xander stood alone in the library for a moment,

then decided not to take any chances, and moved the card catalogue in front of the door. For the first time, Xander was grateful that Giles had resisted the numerous implorations of Ms. Calendar to convert to an online catalogue like every other library in the universe.

*Good. Now I'm safe.*

Then the door opened and Buffy walked in, moving around the catalogue.

*Stupid stupid stupid. A barricade only works against doors that don't open both ways.*

"Alone at last," Buffy said. She was wearing a black raincoat that was tied shut. She was wearing high-heeled shoes.

She didn't appear to be wearing anything else.

"Buff!" Xander said, getting his breathing under control. "Give me a heart attack . . ."

"Oh, I'm gonna give you more than that," she said. And she had on that smile.

As she approached, Xander backed away from her, eventually stumbling onto the staircase to the stacks. Buffy moved closer, fiddling with the belt to the raincoat.

"Buffy, for the love of God, don't open that raincoat."

"Come on," she said, "it's a party. Aren't you gonna open your present?"

"It's not that I don't want to," Xander said quickly. *God, I want to.* "Sometimes the remote, impossible possibility that you might like me was all that sustained me. But not now. Not like this. This isn't real to you. You're only here because of a spell. I mean, if I thought you had one clue what it would mean to me . . . But you don't, so I can't."

*I can't believe I just said that.*

The smile fell from Buffy's face. This would've been a good thing, except it was replaced with anger.

Xander had seen Buffy angry. Her jaw would set in a determined manner and her lips would purse. It was the look she had on her face when she ground the bones of the Master to a sticky paste and when she hacked Ms. French into tiny bits. The classic *I'm the Slayer and you're dead meat* look.

That wasn't the look she had on her face now.

Now her eyes widened and her cheeks flushed. This was what Glenn Close looked like in *Fatal Attraction.*

"So you're saying this is all a game?"

*Oh, no.* "A game? I—no—"

"You make me feel this way and then you reject me? What am I, a toy?"

"Buffy, please, calm down," Xander said, suddenly very nervous. Whether or not this was her usual state of anger, the last thing he wanted was a peeved Slayer.

"I'll calm down when you explain yourself!"

"Get away from him," came a voice from the front of the library. "He's mine!"

It was Amy, though not with Giles and Ms. Calendar. *Which means they're still off trying to find her when she's right here. Great. Can't Win For Losing Boy strikes again.*

"Oh, I don't think so," Buffy said, sneering. "Xander, tell her."

"What?" He was at a loss, and wasn't sure he should say anything. "I—I—"

"He doesn't have to say," Amy said. "I know what his heart wants."

She started to move toward Xander, but Buffy blocked her. "Funny," the Slayer said, "I know what your face wants."

And then she decked Amy.

*This is bad. This is very bad.*

Buffy whirled around and gave him the Glenn Close look again. "What is this? You're two-timing me?"

*This is very very bad.*

"*Goddess Hecate,*" said Amy from behind Buffy, rising to her feet and gesturing, "*work thy will.*"

"Uh oh," Xander muttered.

Amy's eyes had gone dark as she continued her incantation. "*Before thee let the unclean thing crawl!*"

More of that red fire from the other night burst from Amy's hands and enveloped Buffy.

A moment later, Buffy was nowhere to be seen. Just a raincoat and high-heeled shoes crumpled on the floor.

"Buffy!" he cried. "Oh my God."

*This is very very very bad.*

Naturally, Giles and Ms. Calendar chose that moment to return.

"What just happened?" Giles asked. He noticed the raincoat and heels on the floor. "Buffy—where is she?"

Xander hesitated. *How am I going to tell Giles that I got the Slayer disintegrated?*

Then a very large rat crawled out from the sleeve of the raincoat.

On the one hand, Xander was relieved. Changed into a rat was better than disintegrated.

Not that changed into a rat was anything to leap up and cheer about, either.

As the rat scampered around looking for a corner to crawl into, Giles said, "Oh my God."

Amy glared at the computer teacher. "Why is *she* here?"

Xander snapped, "Can you focus for a minute? You just turned Buffy into a rat!"

"Buffy can take care of herself," Amy said, taking Xander's arm. "Why don't we go someplace private?"

Xander shook her off. "Can you—? I'm not going anywhere until you change her back."

Ms. Calendar then grabbed his other arm. "You heard him. So why don't you just undo your little magic trick and get lost?"

"Who made you Queen of the World?" Amy asked. "You're old enough to be—"

"Well, what can I say?" Ms. Calendar said with a cattiness Xander wouldn't have previously given her credit for. "I guess Xander's too much man for the pimple squad."

Amy started fuming. Then her eyes went black again.

*"Goddess Hecate, to you I pray, make thi—"*

She was cut off by Xander clamping his hand over her mouth. As her eyes returned to normal, Xander cried, "Quit with the Hecate!"

Giles finally got into it, grabbing both student-turned-witch and Gypsy-turned-teacher and guiding them toward the desk. "You two sit. Be quiet." He turned to Xander. "We have to catch the Buffy rat."

As Amy and Ms. Calendar slowly sat down opposite each other, Xander looked around. He saw the rat dash behind the new-periodical bookcase by the door. "Oooh, there!" He ran over and peered in the very skinny area between it and the wall. "Good Buffy. Just . . ."

He heard someone behind him. Thinking it was Giles, Xander turned—

Only to be punched in the jaw by Oz.

As Xander collapsed to the floor in a heap, Oz shook his hand up and down. "That kinda hurt."

"Kinda?" Xander said, furious. Today of all days, he didn't need Oz to be Macho Man. "What was that for?"

"I was on the phone all night listening to Willow cry about you. Now I don't know exactly what happened, but I was left with a very strong urge to hit you."

Then Oz reached out his hand to help him up. Xander accepted it, his anger crumbling to dust. He couldn't really say he didn't deserve it. As he rose with Oz's aid, he said, "I didn't touch her, I swear."

"Xander," Giles prompted. "Buffy?"

Nodding, Xander once again peered behind the bookcase, but he couldn't find the rat.

At Oz's confused look, Xander explained, "Amy turned her into a rat."

"Oh," Oz said. Xander suspected that that would be the extent of Oz's reaction. *Talk about a temperament ideally suited for living on the Hellmouth.*

Giles was also looking around. "I don't see her." He turned to Xander. "If anything happens to her I'll—" He cut himself off, and Xander was suddenly grateful he didn't hear the rest of it. "Just go home," Giles said, as angry as Xander had ever heard him. "Lock yourself away. You're only going to cause more problems here. Amy, Jenny, and I will try and break the spells." Then he turned to Oz. "Oz, if you could aid us in finding, um, Buffy."

"Sure, absolutely," Oz said.

Xander started to say something. He wasn't sure what—an apology, maybe—but Giles wouldn't even let him speak. "Just go," the Watcher said, back in that low, dangerous tone. "Get out of my sight."

Sighing, Xander got out of his sight.

Cordelia had no idea how she had survived this day. It was like every girl in the school hated her.

*Maybe,* she thought, *it's one of those stupid Hellmouth-ish things Buffy's always trying to fix.*

She went to her locker to put away her books for the night, then planned to go to the library to see if Giles could be any help.

When she got there, though, she found herself surrounded. It seemed like every girl—and most of the female faculty—were gathered around, and they all stared at her like she was, well, something hateful.

"Okay, what now, you don't like my locker combination?"

Harmony stepped forward. "It's not right. You never loved him. You just *used* him. You make me sick."

"Hey, Harmony, if you need to borrow my Midol, just ask," Cordelia said, suddenly nervous. *This is more than just a general wig-out.*

Harmony then slapped Cordelia. Stunned, Cordelia couldn't respond at first. Then Katie slammed her into the locker.

*This is* definitely *more than just a general wig-out.*

Dori grabbed at her. Kimberley yanked her hair. Harmony slapped her again. A girl from Health class pulled on her arm. Laura tried to bite her. A sophmore scratched her.

Cordelia found herself cringing on the floor, fighting off an attack of teenaged girls.

Then the cafeteria matron took a swing at her with a rolling pin.

*Oh God, I'm gonna die.* Cordelia hadn't been this scared since that invisible chick tied her to her May Queen throne and threatened to slash her face open. Buffy saved her then. *So where is Little Miss Chosen One when I need her?*

"You thought you could do better? Is that it?" Harmony asked.

"No, I," Cordelia stammered. "I—"

Gwen snarled. "We'll knock that snotty attitude right out of you!"

Katie suddenly shrieked, "It's him! It's him!"

Several of the girls ran off to Xander, who had just entered the hallway. He looked like a deer in headlights for a second, then he ran toward Cordelia.

For her part, Cordelia tried to get up, but then Laura knocked her to the ground again.

Xander waded through and pulled Cordelia up into his arms, fighting off his adoring public as he went. Right now, Cordelia didn't care that she hated him. She buried her head in his shoulder and started crying.

After a minute, they were outside. Xander let go of her. "I think we—"

They turned a corner to find another mob. This one was led by Willow.

"Lost them," Xander finished in a much quieter tone.

Willow was holding an axe.

"I should have known I'd find you with her," Willow said, snarling like some spurned soap opera character.

"Will, come on," Xander said, "you don't want to hurt me."

"Oh no? You don't know how hard this is for me. I love you so much, I'd rather see you dead than with her!"

*Of all the times for Willow to get a backbone,* Cordelia thought, *it had to be now?*

Then the other mob, the one led by Harmony, came up behind them. Just as Willow swung at Xander with the axe, Harmony stopped her.

*That's it, stand by your man,* Cordelia thought as she and Xander took advantage of the impromptu catfight that broke out to run away.

Rupert Giles ran his hand through his thinning hair, cursing all things teenaged. Ever since his own youthful indiscretions with the occult had come out, he would have thought that the implicit lesson would have been learned by Buffy and her chums. *Apparently, though, not by Xander.* He went right on ahead and did the same stupid thing Giles had done twenty years earlier. The summoning of the demon Eyghon had resulted at the time in one death, and more recently in two more deaths, and also had put Buffy and Jenny in grave danger. If Giles couldn't figure out a way to reverse this idiotic love spell, the consequences now had the potential to be far worse.

Part of him couldn't remain too angry at Xander. The boy had, after all, saved Buffy's life when the Master left her for dead in a pool of water. He had been through more than any teenager who wasn't a Slayer had any right to, and had not only remained sane, but steadfastly loyal to the cause of Slaying in general and to Buffy in particular.

*If he only weren't such an impulsive fool.*

None of that, however, changed the fact that the Slayer was now a rat, and Giles needed to do something about that, and fast.

To Amy, who was presently sitting morosely in a chair, he said, "You must have botched the ritual so that Cordelia's necklace actually protected her from the spell. That one should be easily reversible. Where did you learn animal transformation?"

"Why did you send Xander away?" she asked. "He needs me."

Jenny, who was pacing, snorted. "That's a laugh."

"He loves me," Amy insisted. "We look into each other's souls."

"No one can love two people at once. What we have is real."

Giles had had more than enough. "Instead of making me ill, why doesn't one of you try to help me?" Both Amy and Jenny had mystical training and abilities. He kept hoping those instincts would come to the fore, but they were swimming upstream against the power of Amy's spell.

Amy leaned back, folded her arms, and pouted in

that depressingly adolescent manner of teenage girls. "You have no idea what I'm going through."

"I know it's not love," Giles snapped. "It's obsession—selfish, banal obsession. Now Xander has put himself in very great danger. If you cared at all about him, you'd help me save him rather than twittering on about your feelings. Now let's get to work." He turned to look behind him. "Jenny—"

But Jenny was gone.

"Great," Giles muttered.

# CHAPTER 6

It took over an hour to finally lose the mob, which had abandoned the catfight and joined forces in trying to pursue Xander and Cordelia. Xander had no idea what their actual plan was. Given that they were a mob, they probably didn't have one.

Xander remembered what mobs did in movies. He also remembered the riots that they'd discussed in history class. Then he ran faster.

By the time they reached Revello Drive, the sun had set. "Now I think we lost them," Xander said.

Cordelia had remained unusually quiet as they ran the streets of Sunnydale avoiding anyone remotely female, but now that they had put the estrogen brigade behind them, she exploded. "Xander, what's going on? Who died and made you Elvis?"

As they came in sight of the house numbered 1630,

Xander said, "There's Buffy's house. Let's get inside. I'll explain later." This was probably the safest place to go, except maybe Giles's place. But that was farther away, and the owner was back at school. Xander's own house would be the first place they'd look.

Luckily, Buffy's mother wasn't working late at the gallery or anything like that. *First thing that's gone right in days,* Xander thought.

"Xander. Cordelia?" Joyce Summers said, letting them in. "What happened? Why are you all scratched up? Where's Buffy?"

Xander hesitated. "She's, um, around."

Joyce led them into the kitchen. "Well, sit down and tell me about it." She turned to Cordy. "Why don't you run upstairs and grab some bandages out of the bathroom?"

Cordelia nodded and ran upstairs.

Xander fell more than sat into one of the chairs at the kitchen table. The strain of running from a mob of love-crazy teenage girls was catching up.

*Well, at least things can't get any worse.*

"Let me get you something to drink," Joyce said. "Are you in the mood for cold or hot?"

That required more thought than Xander was willing to engage in just at the moment. "I, uh—"

Buffy's mom moved closer and put her hands on his shoulders. "I think it's more of a *hot* night, don't you?"

*Oh no. Oh no no no no no.*

Xander dropped his head to the table. It hit with what Xander figured to be a very hollow thud.

"Whatever," he said, defeated.

Joyce started massaging his shoulders. Despite

everything, it actually felt kind of nice. "Goodness," she said, "you are so tense."

"What are you doing?" came Cordy's outraged voice from behind him. "Make me yak!"

"Cordelia, go back upstairs, this is between us," Joyce said angrily.

*Here we go again.*

"Gross. I think not," Cordy said, and pulled the older woman off Xander and shoved her toward the back door and outside.

"What're you doing? Take your hands off of me!" Joyce Summers cried, but Cordy got the upper hand and closed and locked the door.

"And keep your mom-aged mitts off my boyfriend!"

Xander allowed himself a glimmer of hope at that.

"Former!" she added, and Xander sighed.

She turned back to him. "Why has everyone gone insane?"

"Insane?" Xander asked, resenting that particular word choice. *Weird* would've been fine, but *insane* was unfair. "Is it so impossible for you to believe that other women find me attractive?"

"The only way you could get girls to want you would be witchcraft."

"That is such a——" Xander started, then cut himself off. "Well, yeah, okay, good point."

Then a rock went flying through the window of the back door. That was followed by the hand of Joyce Summers trying to find and open the lock. "Xander, honey? Let Joycie in. Let Joycie in!"

Xander and Cordelia exchanged a glance, then ran

out to the hallway and upstairs to Buffy's room. *If nothing else, there are weapons up there.*

Shutting the door behind him, Xander breathed out a sigh of relief.

*Well,* he thought, *at least things can't get any worse.*

He went over to the window and looked out. The streets were empty, aside from one car driving by. "Good. The mob still hasn't found us. We should be safer up—"

Suddenly, Angel, game face on, leaned in through the window from outside, grabbed Xander by the lapels, smiled, said, "Works in theory," then yanked Xander out onto the angled roof of the first floor.

"Xander!" Cordelia cried.

Angel pulled Xander close. "Where's Buffy?"

"Cordy, get out of here!" Xander yelled, hoping Cordelia had the brains to listen.

Then Angel threw Xander off the roof. Xander managed to land feet first and bend his knees with the impact, and so didn't actually break anything, though his ankles and knees were now killing him, and he stumbled and sprawled on his back.

A second later, Angel landed gracefully next to him.

"Perfect," the vampire said with a grin as he grabbed Xander and pulled him up. "I wanted to do something special for Buffy—actually, *to* Buffy—but this is so much better."

Not willing to go down without a fight, Xander kneed Angel. When Xander tried to run, though, the vampire grabbed him and flipped him over onto the lawn. Angel then once again grabbed Xander by the lapels and pulled him close. Baring his fangs, he said,

"If it's any consolation, I feel very close to you right now."

Before he could actually take a bite, though, a hand grabbed Angel and threw him off to the side.

"Buffy? How—"

But it wasn't Buffy. Buffy was probably still wandering around Sunnydale High in search of cheese.

It was Drusilla.

"Don't fret, kitten. Mommy's here."

And she smiled.

It was just like all the other girls' smiles. Except, of course, with fangs.

Xander felt a chill that went all the way to his socks. It never occurred to him that the spell would also affect vampires. And Drusilla wasn't just any old female vampire: she was also completely, totally nuts.

Angel got up, furious. "I don't know what you're up to, Dru, but it doesn't amuse!"

Drusilla helped Xander up and stood protectively between him and Angel. "If you harm one hair on this boy's head . . ."

"You've got to be kidding," Angel said with a sadistic laugh. "Him?"

"Just because I finally found a real man . . ."

Angel shook his head. "I guess I really did drive you crazy." He then seemed to fade in the background and disappear, like he used to do in the old days when he'd show up to give Buffy a mysterious warning.

Drusilla turned back to Xander who, for his part, was as scared as he'd ever been in his life. And that was some very stiff competition.

"Your face is a poem," Drusilla said in a dreamy voice. "Oooooh, I can read it."

"Really? It doesn't say, 'spare me' by any chance?"

She put her fingers on his lips. "Shhhh. How do you feel about eternal life?"

"We couldn't just start with coffee? A movie maybe?"

Just as Drusilla leaned in to do out of love what Angel had been about to do out of hate, angry voices sounded out from behind.

"There he is!"

"Get him!"

Xander had never been so happy to see a lust-crazed mob in his life.

Drusilla and Xander were quickly separated by a gaggle of women who tore at Xander's clothes, reached for his hair, and generally tried to rip him to pieces.

*Okay, maybe "happy" is the wrong word . . .*

"Mine! He's mine!"

"No, mine!"

Then there was Willow with the axe. "All you had to do was love me!"

Before she could bring the axe down, she was bodyslammed by Cordelia.

Cordy managed to grab Xander and lead him to the house. Luckily, the members of the mob couldn't agree on who was Xander's true love, and so kept fighting one another rather than focusing on Xander himself. So Cordelia and Xander managed, barely, to get into the house safely.

Angelus watched with amusement as the women fought over Xander Harris. Now it all made sense.

Obviously, someone had cast a love spell on Harris that made every woman in Sunnydale fall for him.

The vampire laughed. *Oh, this is just too perfect. I couldn't have devised a better torture for Harris if I tried.*

Angelus generally considered Harris and the other toadies Buffy had gathered to herself to be useless. The only ones that really concerned him were the Watcher and Buffy herself. True, Rosenberg showed great potential, and that Calendar woman was a danger, but they were minor threats at best. Harris, though, was less than nothing.

Still, Buffy cared about the gangly little guy for some inexplicable reason, so anything that made him miserable was all right with Angelus.

The only problem, of course, was Dru. However, now that the party had moved into the house, all would be well.

Harris and the Chase girl had locked the door behind them, but Dru led a procession to the back door, which she knocked off its hinges.

The other women all barreled in, but Dru was stopped by what appeared to be an invisible barrier.

"Ah, sorry Dru," Angelus said with another laugh as he drifted closer. "Guess you're not invited." Vampires, after all, could only enter a home if they were invited in. While Buffy had done so for Angel a year earlier when they were being chased by the Three—*back when the drunken Irish gentleman was in charge of this body*—Dru had never had that privilege.

So she couldn't get in.

"Come on, Dru, let's go home, shall we? Sometimes, the Hellmouth just does our work for us."

"But Xander's in there!" she cried plaintively.

"Dru, dear—don't make me use force."

Cordelia locked the door behind her and Xander, then turned to see Mom Summers holding a very large knife.

"It's never gonna work for us, Xander. We have to end it."

Both Cordelia and Xander then ran for the basement. Xander shut and locked the door behind him, then started looking around.

Shaking her head, Cordelia said, "Déjà vu much?" This very basement was where the two of them had started out as a couple. *Like I needed a reminder?* she thought. "Here's another reason not to date you. People are always trying to kill me when I'm with you. So, what do we do now, wait for Buffy to come?"

Xander picked up a hammer, a nail, and a slat of wood. "I wouldn't hold my breath," he muttered, then started nailing the piece of wood over the door.

*Great, it's Night of the Living Dead Psycho Women.* Behind the door, Cordelia could hear the entire female population of Sunnydale pounding on it. *I can't believe this is happening to me. What did I do to deserve this?*

"Give me a nail," Xander said as he finished hammering one board into place.

She handed him one and said, "If we die in here . . ."

"None of this would have happened if you hadn't

broken up with me. But no, you're so desperate to be popular."

Cordelia was amazed. "Me? I'm not the one who embraced the black arts just to get girls to like me. Well, congratulations, it worked."

As Xander hammered in another nail, he said, "It would've worked fine, except your hide's so thick not even magic can penetrate it."

Feeling her jaw drop, Cordelia grabbed Xander by the arm. She had just thought Xander was being his usual moron self. It never occurred to her . . . "You mean, the spell was for *me?*"

Suddenly, a large knife cut through the door. Cordelia screamed. She turned and ran down the stairs, Xander right behind her. She could hear the door being splintered.

Once they reached the basement, an arm went crashing through the window near the ceiling. Some of the girls were trying to get in that way.

"Oh my God," Cordelia cried.

"Stay behind me!" Xander said. He was wielding a giant wrench.

*Oh, great,* Cordelia thought, *that'll hold 'em off for at least two-and-a-half seconds.*

And the mob closed in . . .

# CHAPTER 7

Oz had to admit that his life had certainly changed since he met Willow. Not that he objected to these changes. For one thing, he now had a girlfriend, and an exceedingly cool one at that. For another, Willow's friends were pretty helpful when Oz's cousin's bite turned him into a werewolf. For a third, he finally got some explanation for why this town was so weird.

And he got to do things like steal weapons from army bases and chase people who'd been transformed into rats.

The latter was proving to be more difficult than Oz would have originally thought, once the rat in question left the library. Oz checked around, then heard somebody curse.

Following the noise, he saw Chris, one of the guys in his history class. "Yo, Oz, you see that?"

"See what?" Oz asked.

"This big ol' rat just ran down the basement, man."

"Wow," Oz deadpanned.

Chris shook his head. "Man, don't nothin' faze you?"

Oz shrugged. "Not since I found out that vampires are real. After that, everything kinda pales in significance."

Chris shook his head, laughed, and walked off, obviously not believing a word of it. "Whatever, man. Watch out for the rat."

As soon as Chris was out of sight, Oz went straight for the stairs to the boiler room.

"Hey, Buffy?" Oz called out. He didn't want to turn the lights on, as the rat would run from that much brightness. Luckily, he found a flashlight hanging from a wall on the staircase. Turning it on kept him from tripping on anything, but of the rat there was no sign.

Oz heard a cat meow and hiss at one point, but he heard nothing ratlike.

Idly, Oz wondered if the custodian was in the habit of putting rat traps down here.

The theme from *Ben* going through his head, Oz continued his search. "Here, Buffy . . ."

Giles had dragged Amy, first to her locker to retrieve her spellbook and other components, then to the chemistry lab where she had performed the original ritual. After asking her three times, she finally consented to redraw the female symbol on the floor while Giles prepared the herbs.

"Right," he said when all was in readiness. "Go on. You first." They had agreed that she would reverse the animal transformation, while Giles would reverse the love spell. This was mainly because Amy herself refused to do the latter. Giles, in no mood to argue, decided to try his own hand at it.

*I've successfully spellcasted a few times lately, including once with Amy. Not bad for a chap who swore he'd never go near the occult again twenty years ago, eh?*

When the water started boiling, and a rather pungent odor permeated the air, Amy read from the book. As she spoke, Giles dropped a tuft of rodent hair into the mixture.

*"Goddess of creatures great and small, I conjure thee to withdraw. Hecate! I hereby license thee to depart!"*

The beaker roiled, and a puff of red smoke emerged from it.

*That's one down,* Giles thought, hoping that she didn't bollix it up like she did the love spell, and transform Buffy into a newt.

Holding the necklace Xander had given Cordelia in his hand, Giles took the spellbook from a now-sulking Amy and read.

*"Diana, goddess of love, be gone. Hear no more thy siren's song."*

He dropped the necklace into the beaker. The manifestation this time was on a much greater scale, filling the room briefly with a bright, red light.

Then the room was dark once again.

"What—what happened?" Amy asked, sounding confused.

Giles took that as a good sign indeed.

The first thing Buffy realized was that the cheese she had been about to consume was in a rat trap.

The second thing she realized was that, for the first time in a few days, she could think straight.

The third was that she was completely naked.

She was standing next to some crates. On the other side of those crates stood Oz, holding a flashlight. To his credit, and Buffy's relief, he flicked off the flashlight as soon as he saw the state of Buffy's dress—or lack of dress, as the case may be.

"Hi, Oz," she said weakly.

"Hi."

"I seem to be having a slight case of nudity here."

Oz pointed at her and smiled. "But you're not a rat. So call it an up side."

Buffy found she couldn't argue with that.

"Do you think maybe you can get me some clothing?"

"Yes, I can," Oz said, turning to head upstairs. "Just don't go anywhere."

"*Really* not an issue," she said with feeling.

*So this is it,* Xander thought. *We're going to die.*

*Of all the ways I expected to go, being mauled by a group of lust-maddened women while curled in the fetal position in Buffy's basement wasn't exactly high on the list.*

And then, suddenly, it got quiet.

Xander looked up to see that all the women—Willow, Harmony, Katie, Gwen, Laura, Ms. Calendar, Buffy's mom, and all the others—were kind of standing around looking dazed.

"What," Joyce Summers stammered, "what did we—?"

Cordelia put on her May Queen smile and said, "Boy, that was the best scavenger hunt *ever!*"

"Scavenger hunt?"

Buffy was shaking her head and laughing as she and Xander walked down the quad the following morning. Xander was recounting the story from his own perspective, including the rather nasty attack from Angel. He had just come to the end.

"Your mom seemed to buy it," Xander said defensively.

"So she says. I think she's just so wigged at hitting on one of my friends that she's repressing. She's getting pretty good at that." Buffy thought about this for a second. "I should probably start worrying."

Xander smiled, then sighed. "Well, I'm back to being incredibly unpopular."

"It's better than everybody trying to axe murder you, right?"

*Gotta give her that one.* "Mostly. But Willow won't even talk to me."

Buffy shot him a look. "Any particular reason she should?"

Xander asked plaintively, "How much groveling are we talking here?"

"Oh, a month at least. Xander, c'mon, I mean, this was worse for her than anyone. She loved you before you invoked the great roofie spirit. The rest of us . . ."

This time Xander shot her a look. He'd been so busy giving his side of the story that he hadn't gotten Buffy's. "You remember, huh?"

"Oh yeah," she said with a nasty smile. "I remember coming on to you. I remember begging you to undress me. And then a sudden need for cheese." A pause, then: "I also remember that you didn't."

"Need cheese?"

"Undress me. It meant a lot to me, what you said."

*Well, I salvaged something from this mess, at least.* "C'mon, Buffy, I couldn't take advantage of you like that. Okay, for a minute, it was touch and go there, but—"

"You came through, Xander. There might be some hope for you yet."

With another sigh, Xander said, "Well, tell that to Cordelia."

"You're on your own, there."

Cordelia had intended to face the next day as another new day. Another ordinary day at her ordinary school. She was going to pretend that the previous day just didn't happen. No love spells, no geeky losers trying to win her back, none of that.

She was walking with Harmony, Dori, Katie, Kimberley, and Laura, talking about guys. Everything was perfectly ordinary, as per the plan.

*So why does it all feel wrong?*

"Cody Weinberg called me at home last night," Harmony squealed.

Cordelia was impressed. "Cody Weinberg? The one with the Three-fifty SL?"

"The very one. Said he's thinking of asking me to the pledge dance on Thursday."

"That's so huge," Cordelia said. And it was. Cody was quite a catch. Not Cordelia's type, really—she hadn't been able to bear dating a blond since the Sven disaster during Cultural Exchange Week—but it was great for Harmony.

"Yeah. There's just two other girls he's gonna ask first, and if they refuse, then I—"

Before she could continue, Harmony literally bumped into Xander.

*Oh great, here we go.*

"Watch it!" Harmony said.

Expecting him to wig out or something, Cordelia was surprised with how meekly he said, "Sorry."

Then he just moved on.

Harmony called out to his back. "God, I'm glad your mom stopped working the drive-thru long enough to dress you."

Cordelia saw Xander hesitate, then keep walking.

And then she figured it out.

There had been something wrong about all of this, going back to when Harmony and the others blew her off just because she was dating Xander.

*Who are they, anyhow?*

Cordelia Chase was the trendsetter. People lined up to see what she was wearing so they'd know what the right thing to wear *was*. And what she did was, by definition, cool.

*So why am I busting my aerobicized butt to please these little twerps?*

And then she thought about a beautiful silver heart

necklace, and a guy who was willing to dabble in black magic to get her back.

"That reminds me," Harmony babbled on, "did you *see* Jennifer's backpack? It's so trying—"

"Harmony, shut up," Cordelia said.

Harmony stopped walking and stared at Cordelia in something like shock. The others behind her did the same.

Down the quad, so did Xander.

*Good. He should hear this.*

"You know what you are, Harmony? You're a sheep."

"I'm not a sheep," Harmony said meekly.

"You're a *sheep*. All you ever do is what everyone else does, just so you can say you did it first. And here I am, scrambling for your approval, when I'm *way* cooler than you are because I'm *not* a sheep. I do what I want to do, and I wear what I want to wear, and you know what? I'll date whoever the hell I want to date."

Xander brightened.

"No matter how lame he is." Xander's face fell a bit.

With that, she turned on her heel, and walked straight for Xander. She grabbed his hand, and pulled him along, not breaking stride.

As soon as they turned a corner, she realized what, exactly, she had just done.

"Oh God, oh God."

"You're gonna be okay," Xander said, talking like she was about to jump off a roof. "Just keep walking."

"Oh God, what have I done? They're never gonna speak to me again."

"Sure they are," Xander said confidently. "If it helps, whenever we're around them, you and I can fight a lot."

She looked up at him gratefully. "You promise?"

Smiling, Xander said, "You can pretty much count on it."

# TONIGHT, PART 4

*The funny thing is,* Xander thought, *Cordy's been just about the only stable thing in my life lately.*

After Cordelia decided to give the relationship another shot, they had actually done fairly well. Throughout all that followed—Angel, Jenny, Kendra—Xander and Cordelia had stayed together.

*Arguing constantly, but we've stayed together,* he thought.

The phone rang, startling Xander. He picked it up. "Joe's Pizza, Joe's not here."

"Xander, it's me," Cordelia said. "We're on for tomorrow morning, right?"

Blinking in confusion, Xander said, "Huh?"

"Tomorrow. We're on, right?"

"I'm missing something here, Cordy."

"So what else is new? Look, I'm going to pick you up around eleven. That'll give you plenty of time to slack around and sleep late like you always do on Saturdays, even though the mall will be *packed* by then."

"The mall? Why are we going to the mall?" Xander felt like he had slept through a meeting or something.

"He*llo?* To get you some new clothes to replace those Salvation Army castoffs you've been embarrassing me in public with. Don't you recall *any*thing I said to you tonight?"

Xander came within a hair of answering that question honestly, but if he'd learned nothing else while dating Cordelia, he knew that telling her you weren't hanging on her every word was the kiss of death. *Or, more to the point, death without the kiss.*

"Right. The mall. No problemo. I am Shopping Guy, hear me roar."

"Good. See you tomorrow at eleven, then."

With that, she hung up. Cordy never wasted time talking on the phone to guys. Phone time was for girls. Serious gossiping, and all that.

Staring at the phone he'd just hung up, he thought back over the vast minefield that had been his love life over the last couple of years.

*A super-strong Vampire Slayer who prefers a vampire to me. A giant praying mantis disguised as the most beautiful substitute bio teacher on record. A five-hundred-year-old killer mummy. And the girl I've spent the last twelve years despising.*

*Oh no, my life's not too surreal . . .*

Sighing and smiling at the same time, he stripped to his boxers, turned out the lights, climbed into bed, and fell asleep.

He dreamed of Buffy Summers.

# ABOUT THE AUTHOR

Born in the Bronx to a pack of wild librarians, **Keith R. A. DeCandido** has been author, editor, musician, critic, anthologist, TV personality, and packager in nine years in the science fiction/fantasy/horror/comics field.

With José R. Nieto, he wrote the Spider-Man novel *Venom's Wrath,* and he and José are working on the sequel *Venom's Rage,* due in 2000. Keith has published over half a dozen short stories in a variety of anthologies, and also assisted Christopher Golden and Nancy Holder in writing *Buffy the Vampire Slayer: The Watcher's Guide.*

Keith has co-edited several acclaimed anthologies, including *OtherWere: Stories of Transformation* (with Laura Anne Gilman), *Urban Nightmares* (with Josepha Sherman), *The Ultimate Alien,* and *The Ultimate Dragon* (both with Byron Preiss and John Betancourt). His other editorial accomplishments range from editing a highly successful line of superhero novels to helping bring legendary science fiction author Alfred Bester back into print.

He is also the percussionist for the Don't Quit Your Day Job Players, a rock/blues/folk/country band that plays regularly at science fiction conventions, where they have oft-times been Musical Guests of Honor, and at New York City clubs. The band's first CD, *TKB,* was released in 1996.

The proprietor of Albé-Shiloh Inc., writing and editorial services, Keith lives in New York City with his lovely and much more talented wife, Marina Frants. You can find out more than you ever needed to know about the pair of them at www.sff.net/people/krad.

"They say young people don't learn
anything in high school nowadays,
but I've learned to be afraid."
—Xander

# BUFFY
## THE VAMPIRE
# SLAYER™

# THE POSTCARDS

Buffy Summers may have missed picture
day at Sunnydale High, but now you
can get your own stash of all-new Slayer
snapshots.

Twenty-two official, full-color photos from
the hit show—all packed into one postcard
gift book.

Available February 1999

Published by Pocket Books

POCKET
BOOKS

2058

"Well, we could grind our enemies into powder with a sledgehammer, but gosh, we did that last night."
— *XANDER*

# BUFFY
### THE VAMPIRE
# SLAYER™

As long as there have been vampires, there has been the Slayer. One girl in all the world, to find them where they gather and to stop the spread of their evil ... the swell of their numbers.

### #1 THE HARVEST

### #2 HALLOWEEN RAIN

### #3 COYOTE MOON

### #4 NIGHT OF THE LIVING RERUN

### THE ANGEL CHRONICLES, VOL. 1

### BLOODED

### THE WATCHER'S GUIDE
(The Totally Pointy Guide for the Ultimate Fan!)

### THE ANGEL CHRONICLES, VOL. 2

Based on the hit TV series created by Joss Whedon

### Published by Pocket Books

1399-08

idea what he might be in for if he challenged the Chosen One.

"Hey look at us," Buffy said with a smile. "We came up with a plan. A good plan."

"Right. We can meet there tonight after it closes."

The smile fell. "No! Bad plan! I have other plans. Dance plans."

The Watcher fixed her with one of the gazes he'd spent years developing, but which only sporadically worked on this particular Slayer.

Buffy leaned back in her chair and sulked. "Canceled plans."

Giles allowed himself a small smile of triumph.

The princess had managed to calm herself down, mainly due to the presence of dear Alexander. With him, she almost felt safe.

Almost.

Still, she lived in constant fear, both of the Guardian of the Seal, and of the Seal itself. She knew that she could never have the normal life she so desperately craved as long as there was a hope of restoring the seal, and as long as the Guardian lived.

But she had to do everything she could to make that life work. This world was glorious, full of so much more than her home in Peru, thousands of miles and five centuries away. She could make a life here.

Sebancaya willing, she could make that life with Xander.

"Okay," Xander said as they walked down the hallway, "I have something to tell you, and it's kind of a secret. And it's a little bit scary."

"You mean, the spell was for me?"
　　　　　　　—Cordelia

Nicholas Brendon plays Xander.

Xander asked Buffy, "You okay?"

"Yeah."

Preparing himself for a five-course meal of crow, Xander said, "Just for the record, you were right, I'm an idiot, and God bless you."

Buffy smiled a no-hard-feelings smile, for which Xander was grateful.

Turning to Giles and Willow, Xander said, "And thank you guys, too."

"Yeah, really," Blayne said. He sounded a bit more together than he had in the cage.

"Pleasure," Giles said.

"I'm really glad you're okay," Willow said to Xander, moving next to him. "It's so unfair how she only went after virgins."

Xander blinked. "What?"

"I mean, here you guys are, doing the right thing— the smart thing—when a lot of other boys your age—"

Blayne straightened up and interrupted. "Flag down on that play, babe. I am *not*—"

Giles smiled and said, "That's the She-Mantis's *modus operandi*—she only preys on the pure."

*Pure. Now I'm "the pure." Whoopee.* Aloud, Xander said, "Well, isn't this a perfect ending to a wonderful day?"

Blayne pointed at each of them in turn. "My dad's a lawyer. Anybody repeats this to anybody, they're gonna find themselves facing a lawsuit."

*For what, definition of character?* Xander thought. "Blayne," he said, "shut up."

"I don't think it's bad," Willow said with a smile. "I think it's really—"

"Well anyway," she said after a moment, starting to take the jacket off, "you can have your jacket back."

He held up a hand to stop her. "Looks better on you." And then he ran his hand along the collar for a moment.

It suddenly got very warm in the Bronze.

Angel then walked off. Buffy looked after him, long after he had disappeared from sight.

"Oh boy."

Principal Flutie had found a new biology teacher to take Dr. Gregory's place. He was taller than his predecessor, with less hair, and he had all the physical presence of a dead plant. Buffy hadn't really appreciated Dr. Gregory's lecturing skills until she had to listen to this guy—whose name she couldn't even remember—drone on.

"All midterm papers will be exactly six pages long. No more. No less. One-third of your grade will be dependent on those papers. No more. No less."

*His tone doesn't change,* she thought with horror at the coming doldrums of the rest of the term. She had just started to get into bio, but she suspected that this teacher would drain that interest right out of her.

She looked over at the table next to her. Xander was trying hard to pay attention and failing miserably. Buffy figured that was residual guilt combined with a desire never to be taken in by a giant praying mantis again. Willow, on the other hand, looked like she was fighting to keep her eyes open.

*Classic danger sign,* she thought. *If the teacher's even boring Will, he must be a loser.*